Praise for Animalia:

"Pam Jones's *Animalia* is like a metaphysical *Harry and the Hendersons* if it had been directed by Michael Haneke. In this map to Eden, Jones writes in simple sentences that add up to pack a big punch. *Animalia* is a beautiful, wholly original meditation on what it means to be the awful animal that is Human."

— Jesi Bender, author of *Kinderkrankenhaus* and *The Book of the Last Word*

"A wonderfully strange and fascinating observation on family and spirituality, on what makes us human and what makes us wild."

— Tomas Moniz, author of *All Friends Are Necessary* and *Big Familia*

"With haunting and beautiful prose, Pam Jones' *Animalia* weaves a lyrical, Kafkaesque tale of three long-missing children who return home as adults, claiming to have found Eden. Jones explores the primal nature of humanity and our longing to return to innocence that can never truly be achieved. A spellbinding exploration of the philosophy of nature and the price of reaching for utopia."

— Eric Z. Weintraub, author of *South of Sepharad*

"*Animalia* by Pam Jones is a novel completely gorgeous in its primordial, philosophical energies. In this best of all possible Edens, which unflinchingly ropes in the worst of all possible impulses, Jones's tense, sorcerous narrative is a lamp unto our feet, a light neon-red and warning."

— Vincent James, author of *Acacia, a Book of Wonders*

Also by Pam Jones

A Carnival of Birds
The Arizona Room
Anointed
The Joyful Mysteries
Ivy Day
Andermatt County: Two Parables

Denver, Colorado

Published in the United States by:
Spaceboy Books LLC
1627 Vine Street
Denver, CO 80206
www.readspaceboy.com

Cover features image from the Harley Bestiary, ca. 1230-1240 AD, Harley MS, British Museum and by Joe from Pixabay

ISBN: 978-1-951393-37-3
First printed July 2024

To my parents

"Esteemed Gentlemen of the Academy! You show me the honour of calling upon me to submit a report to the Academy concerning my previous life as an ape."

— Franz Kafka, "A Report to an Academy"

"I said in mine heart concerning the estate of the sons of men, that God might manifest them, and that they might see that they themselves are beasts."

— Ecclesiastes 3:18

They Reappear

The people who emerged from the woods and onto the pavement were two males and one female. It had been a considerable length of time since any of them had felt it necessary to walk upright, but they managed it, once they stepped from grass to sidewalk, and found that they bore up well along some distance, about three miles. Their gait was stiff and slow, their legs widely spread, and their feet made wet slapping sounds that were alien against the very early quiet of the morning. It would be another hour before dawn.

It would be another hour before dawn and they were guided along these solid shut places, apartment complexes, markets, gas stations, restaurants offering dollar menus, martial arts studios, much in the same way that they had been guided from them two decades prior. Many of these places had not been there when the two males and the one female were last among such things.

They stopped at a park that was thickly wooded, in between two apartment buildings. For a minute, they stood beneath the canopy and smelled the air around them. A male remarked that he had taken tennis lessons in this park once, years ago. The female and the other male nodded. It had been the first English, nay, the first spoken language that he had used in many years, the first that his companions had heard in as much time. It was understood, without words, that here was where the parties would split. A purplish day was suggesting itself when they reached the park's baseball field, where an entrance and exit was, not the main one at the parking lot. This one led into a neighborhood of small houses, limestone and clapboard, numbered at the curb.

It was into this neighborhood that three naked individuals stepped and felt themselves shift according to memory, a dim recollection of having walked on two legs all the time, rather than use their four limbs. Another recollection, one of covering up. They had not worn clothes in as many years as they had not spoken. The elements had changed them. They were furred and clawed, and the males were bearded. The female was bare-breasted. Their sexes were stark against their pubic matting.

They had not quite left the park when the female called them back, a quick hoot. She pointed to a bench and its flowers, situated across from the baseball diamond. In spring and summer, it had the look of a heavenly throne, surrounded as it was by the mopheads of blue hydrangeas. They nodded, spectatorial clouds over the empty seat. The males and female went to work gathering blooms, using force or their teeth against the branches, ignoring the plaque fixed into the bench's back slats. IN LOVING MEMORY OF OUR CHILDREN. Beneath that, in smaller letters, were six names. WE DEDICATE THIS SPOT TO ALONSO, ALLRED, CLARE, EVANDER, JULIAN, and MARY KATHLEEN. There was a date: MAY 15. There was no year. There was no further message.

When they finished, they stood back with their arms full of blue and white foam, dripping petals. Here was when they noticed the plaque, found their names. Here was when the female spoke, articulate, if hoarse. "They think we died," she pronounced.

The males nodded.

The male who had not yet spoken put in, "Just our first names." He pointed, the nail long.

As it happened, three of their number were dead. Three of their number were dead and they three had gone on, as they had said they would do, when half of their number had decimated. Their years away had made them matter-of-fact; they had not wept when two females and one male had not woken. They had done what they said they would do: They had gone on, gone home to see their people, and to inform the families of the deceased. They did not intend to stay for long.

They stripped the bench of its flowers and left the park, each in their own direction. They had said that they would part in this way and would not look back.

They had been three females and three males.

Now they were one female and two males.

Now was the hour when the streetlights turned off.

The female encountered a police car. The officer inside was sleepy, friendly, unconcerned at the sight of a woman, otherwise nude, save for a cloud of hydrangeas. It was still dark and while the woman did look wild, she did not look unhinged or uncivilized. When asked if she needed assistance, the woman said, "No." When asked where she was headed, the woman said, "I'm going home." She gave the address and obliged when the officer trailed her along the sidewalk, for she would not accept a ride, and thanked the officer for waiting until she had gone inside.

There had been a flowerpot on the porch which housed an extra key. It had been there, and the key, these two decades and more.

The males recalled less from life before. Keys and their use eluded them, and their families had not been the kind of people who hid housekeys under flowerpots. One male tried a window and, finding it open, slipped through with ease. The other, with less luck, made do with the round, Grecian concrete head of the birdbath from the garden. First, he squatted to relieve himself in the grass. When he was through, he took the birdbath and knocked it against the sliding glass door until it shattered in its frame. He stepped inside, along and upon the shards, for his feet were padded and too thick to register the cuts.

The female had to wait for her father to wake and, meanwhile, stood over her parents in their bed, observing, smelling. Their house was two-story, their bedroom far from the sun and completely dark, the curtains drawn.

The male who came through the open window did the same. His parents slept on the second story, too. At first, the stairs troubled him; negotiating such small steps in ascension had very nearly caused him to fall, and he made it halfway up, one hand in a wet grip around the banister, the other steadying the flowers under his arm. He spilled blue petals and, when he looked, saw that he'd made a trail starting from the kitchen. Finally, he resorted to the usual way, flowers between his jaws, all four limbs at work, galloping to the top and rising on two legs in silence. He did not recall the use of keys and their locks, but he did know what his mother and father smelled like. Tracking the odor, he found them, still asleep.

The other male gathered his flowers, righted himself, stilled, listened overhead for a bedroom door opening, shutting, footfalls in quick succession, gasping, cursing—

When the parents saw their children, it was first their eyes in the dark and nothing else.

David Livingstone said, "I saw two gold flecks. Two round, gold flecks blinking and hovering like that, in the dark. It was still very early. At first, I thought an animal had got into the house. An animal that wasn't our dog. I wasn't entirely awake yet. My wife recognized her first, and I thought she was dreaming. I very nearly told her. I very nearly told her just that. But then she said, JULES. And she was out of bed—"

Marisol Enamorado said, "I knew immediately. It was like we'd been waiting for this day. I woke my husband. We didn't have to turn on the lights, we knew who it was. Alonso was standing there at the end of our bed, like he'd been waiting, too, I thought. He just said, Hi, Mom. Just like that. He was nine the last time we saw him."

Joel McKnight said of his step-son, "Allred was right there, standing on all that broken glass. I admit, my hair stood on end. It took a minute to know who it was. At first glance, here was this naked man, scarred up, hair matted, the smell of him was unbelievable. He looked like the Great Unwashed. He was standing there in the glass as though it didn't bother him. I froze where I was. I wasn't sure if he had a weapon or if he was crazy. His mother was disabling the alarm and I didn't want to frighten her. But he was carrying flowers, all those flowers. His mouth was going, his jaw was working, as though he was trying to make words. I noticed one thing that made everything click. You know how David Bowie had one blue eye and one green eye, or whatever it was? Two different colored eyes? Allred took tennis lessons in the summers, from about ages five to about nine, when he disappeared. Well, at one of his first lessons, he'd caught a tennis ball square in the left eye, and the pupil dilated and fixed that way, and it made him look like he had one green eye and one brown eye. And that's how I knew it was him."

David Livingstone said, "I think she was happy to see us. I believe she was. She didn't seem to know what to do when we went to embrace her. She let us, but she didn't drop the flowers she was hanging onto. She sort of put her nose to our necks, then in our hair. She actually used her hands and brought our heads down so that she could smell us."

Marisol Enamorado said, "We hugged him and he —I suppose you could say he relented. He was stiff. It seemed as though he was being very patient with us. He had to let us do our thing first. I think he was expecting that to want to embrace him—I think he knew it would be the first thing we'd do. And he was tolerant. But, no, I don't think he liked it."

Donna Avery McKnight said, "I'm ashamed to say it, but I saw him and I wanted to call the police. I thought he was a vagrant on drugs. I thought we were being robbed. He looked like a vagrant. My husband had to get ahold of me. He made me stand there to get a proper look at him. He said, It's Al. Al's back. I burst into tears and I ran for him. That scared him. He leapt right out into the backyard. No noise, and so swift, it was like watching a deer. And it was amazing—he'd gone up a tree. Before, he'd never been very strong or coordinated. He wasn't into climbing trees or anything like that. But he got himself up that tree faster than we could think. And then we did have to call the police to coax him to come back down, which he did do, after about an hour."

The female called Julian asked her parents for a pen and a piece of paper. She spoke with great deliberation and clarity, for she did not want anything she said to be lost in confusion. She had, at first, mimed the gesture of writing in a scribble across the air with her finger. Not having used her voice for much more than rudimentary barks and whoops and shouts and yelps, it was a surprise for her to find the act of speech an arduous one. It hurt. The vocal chords protested. Articulation did not keep up with volume, and after watching their daughter mouth the question, and after asking her to repeat herself many times, the female was able to say at slightly more than a whisper, "I'd like a pen and paper, please."

Prior to her disappearance, David Livingstone recalled his daughter having been right-handed. He observed her taking up the pen in her left, as though this were the hand that she had been meant to use all along. He insisted that her school, the local public elementary, had not forced her to change and neither had he and his wife.

They tore a page from a yellow legal pad and set it and the pen at the desk opposite the bed. The female took both and went on all fours to the floor, pen in her fist. She carved letters in approximation of standard fourth-grade cursive.

David Livingstone said, "It'd been so long. I wanted to say something about how the schools don't teach cursive anymore."

His wife took the paper from her when she had finished.

In blocky but correct script were three names and three addresses. They were:

EVANDER - 17 NATURAL SPRING RD.

CLARE - 6 TARSUS RD.

MARY KATHLEEN - 2223 LOWER ALBERT RD.

It was now that the female called Julian rose to her feet in imitation of her parents and informed them in the same voice that sounded, as it did, from the bowels of a large, newly articulate beast, that she ought to inform the families of these three that their children were dead.

Amid the ruckus and the elation and the whirling bewilderment, the parents of the living decided to keep the males separate from the female. It was an instinctive first order of business, as issued by David Livingstone, a retired Marine who had gone to the farthest reaches of civilization and returned with the certainty that he had seen everything. He understood the villainy of men and was the first to admit it when he informed the public and his wife that his decision was founded on his suspicion of some harm having come to his daughter, at the males' hands and appetites. His words, when questioned by the Enamorado and McKnight families, were brief. The volume sufficed: "THEY'RE BOYS."

He put the telephone down and heard his daughter echo from the next room, "They're boys."

He said later, "We are villains. God have mercy, but men are foul. We take and we take. It's our burden. They say a man has a thought of sexual nature every ten minutes. There is not one doubt in my mind that those three ganged up on her. And the other girls, too. Of course, they did. And I'll tell you something else. I can assume that those three, those three who are no longer with us. I think we have our surviving fellows to thank for that."

David Livingstone spoke from experience. As a young man in basic training, he had been an inactive participant to an incident off-base. He would argue that he was merely an observer. In truth, he had been a photographer. A night out, alcohol in excess. The images and its subject do not survive. No one would know and no one would care.

Marisol described her son's homecoming thusly:

Jumanji.

"I guess somebody rolled a five or an eight," she said. "Because there he was."

When Alonso had last been home, been inside of a house, having merely glimpsed them from hilltops and hillsides as burnished flashes, banks of noisy villages, the family had not had a computer. He'd had to make do with going to the library or crossing the street to his friend Alec's house. Alonso's parents were wary of violence, knowing what conscientious objectors knew, that bloodshed was growing more insidious by the day, like a mold in your television set. At the time of their son's disappearance, the Enamorados had not owned a television set, and at present they still do not. Alec's parents, as it turned out, went to the same church as Alonso's and felt the same way as they did. They had read of Rand Miller's *Myst* series, absorbing that, while they were unsure if Miller was a Christian or a Buddhist, its maker was a confirmed pacifist, as they were. There would be no gruesome images. Alonso's father, who talked of his son in the present tense as though nothing had changed, was a great reader and picked up on the inspiration drawn from Jules Verne. They conceded to *Myst* and games like it, approving them for their narratives, objectives, message, language.

He said, "I remember, there are a lot of puzzles, I keep notes, I don't know what I did with them now. I must say, I got into more than I thought I might.

Maybe it's that soundtrack. It actually has a rather relaxing effect, which I wasn't expecting in a video game. And Alonso really likes it."

They had installed a wide, white Mac in the den, which served a dignified ten-year term, before graduating to laptops and phones. The family started when they realized that their son, now returned, did not have a laptop or a phone of his own. The day following Alonso's homecoming, his mother went to the Apple Store near the Arboretum and purchased both. At home, after the initial setups were complete, she learned from a nephew that games were no longer developed in the CD-ROM format, and was directed to the site called Steam, where they were able to find and install Rand Miller's *Myst* series on Alonso's new machine.

"It's a point-and-click game," Marisol said. "There are switches to flip and items to pick up. You have to assemble pages you find into a book that will free one of the sons of the island's creator. Or free the creator's wife. There's nothing alarming in it. But Alonso didn't seem to grasp the objectives. He was content to point-and-click to certain locations, if he liked the music. He'd kind of sit at a certain spot for a while, and then he'd move on once the song was done."

The McKnights brought their son to their general practitioner, so as to avoid any excess attention that they might have found at a hospital.

Allred's stepfather said, "Our first impulse had been to bring Al to his pediatrician. But she had retired and was very frail by that point. And we had to remind ourselves that the patient was now nearly thirty. It would be inappropriate. And we'd known Paul for many years."

The general practitioner had known Allred from the tennis ball incident, having been available to treat it while the pediatrician was out of town at that time for a funeral. It was this same general practitioner that accumulated his observations on the now grown and now changed patient into a brief dossier. In addition to weight and height, he noted that the subject's bodily hair had thickened incrementally and had multiplied, with a focus on the forearms, the legs, the backs of the hands and the tops of the feet. As for the hands and feet themselves, the fingers and toes appeared to have exceeded the usual length found in a modern man, and were found to be adaptable in the act of interchangeable service. For example, the subject, when asked, could pick up and hold a pencil in his right foot and, with a new dexterity, manipulate the pencil as he would in his hand. The subject, when asked, was able to write his name in this way. However, when asked to do the same with his hand, the subject experienced what the general practitioner described as "a mental block" and could not perform the task.

The general practitioner made notes concerning the subject's tolerance for discomfort. Allred Avery-McKnight was administered long-overdue vaccinations for influenza, tetanus and diphtheria, pertussis, human papilloma virus, polio, and rubella. So as to stagger any side-effects, these injections were given over a period of two months.

His mother said, "Previously, it was a whole production just to get him to the doctor's office if he knew that there would be a shot. He cried every time. He cried even if he was putting in an effort not to cry. He had to cover his face when he was little. And then, later on, he had to bring his CD player, so he'd have something to distract him. It didn't matter if you told him that it'd only hurt for a second, or that he was too big for this kind of thing. There would still be tears. We remembered the CD player this time, and he seemed to like that. I think there was an Earth, Wind, & Fire greatest hits collection in there. I don't know if it was Earth, Wind, & Fire that did it, but it was the same as him standing in all those shards of glass. As though getting needles in his arm, plus blood tests, was nothing to him."

Blood tests showed normal readings for white blood cells, and a count of red blood cells (including tests for universal hemoglobin, mean corpuscular volume, and mean corpuscular hemoglobin) ruled out malnutrition and anemia. His platelet count revealed slightly higher numbers, indicating to his parents the possibility of infection. Allred's stepfather had been a hematologist and his mother a phlebotomist. Standard data had sounded the alarum. They demanded tests at once, alternately petting and uttering apologies to their son, who sat throughout these proceedings in a stiff paper gown, without expression, save for his absorption of Earth, Wind, & Fire's greatest hits.

They searched for evidence of sepsis, rabies, hepatitis, e. coli, giardia. They ordered tests for potassium, phosphorus, creatine, chloride, and calcium. They ordered tests for histoplasmosis (known better as cave disease) and the bubonic plague.

Paul asked Allred if he had ever lived in a cave.

The subject said plainly, "No."

Paul asked Allred if he had ever eaten anything that might have been rotten. "Did any meat or plant taste different or funny to you?"

The subject told him, "No."

Paul asked Allred, "Did you eat only plants when you were living outside, out there?"

Again, the subject told him, "No."

Paul asked, "You ate meat sometimes?"

The subject responded in the affirmative.

"But not all the time."

"No."

Paul asked, "What kinds of meat did you eat when you were living out there, outside?"

The subject appeared puzzled by the question. His parents had taken away the CD player and his movements were agitated. The subject paced. He gnawed at the hairs on his knuckles. He had been given clothes, blue jeans and a blue t-shirt that his mother had picked up at a nearby Kohl's while the subject was undergoing tests. He regarded them in their shopping bag with some measure of distrust, as though he would be in violation of some custom unbeknownst to modern man. The blue jeans looked to be the right size. The t-shirt was solid in color, no phrases or images. As for shoes, he had outright refused them. The box, Converse, classic black high tops, he had pushed to one side, and the sneakers leaned to one side of the Kohl's bag, still, like artifacts.

The doctor asked, once the parents had retired to the waiting room, if there had been anything that had happened to make the subject want to leave home.

The subject answered that this was not so.

"Would you say that you were angry with your parents?"

Again, the subject said, "No."

"It wasn't because of your mother's divorce? Or her remarrying at all?"

"No. I love my dad."

"Your stepfather."

"Joel. He's my dad."

"You love Joel?"

"Yes."

"You love your mother, too?"

"Yes."

"Okay. Al, did anyone older than you, and I mean a grown person, did anyone like that ever try to get you to do something that you didn't want to do?"

"No."

The doctor repeated the question. The second time, he added, "Did anyone try to make you leave your home that night? Did anyone come to your window? Or did anyone follow you in the days or weeks beforehand? Like, did anyone trail you home from school?"

Allred Avery-McKnight was six months shy of his thirtieth birthday. He did not recall the necessity of keys or telephones. He recalled the alphabet, but not its complexities. He understood television and radio, in that he understood that the sounds and images were being broadcast from another place and did not originate in the objects themselves; he knew that there were no people in the TV. He knew what a toilet was, though he preferred to relieve himself outdoors. He understood that his family would not appreciate this, and when his parents supplied him with adult diapers, he put them on without complaint and changed them of his own accord when he fouled them.

His vocabulary seemed limited, spare to the point of issuing a Yes or a No, and with little need to elaborate. His comprehension of language remained intact, which suggested to the doctor that the subject's mutism was not only selective but completely reversible.

"You just had to pose the right questions," Paul said.

He asked again if anyone had told the subject to leave his home on the night of his disappearance.

Here, the subject was lost in thought, or so it seemed to the doctor. "It was a question that could only have yielded a Yes or No. But he sat there and kind of stewed about it for a good five minutes. He'd been pulling at the hairs on his arm—and it was thick, more like fur. And he'd been idly kind of pulling at it when a large portion fell out onto his lap. He brushed at himself, as though he were brushing off crumbs, and a whole sheaf came off this time. He continued to do this with the other arm, and with his shoulders and his legs, and in about a minute the floor of my office looked like a dog groomer's, after you get done shaving down a really hairy customer. He asked me if the hair on his head was going to come off like that, too, and I told him that, while it was possible, he'd need to get down to a barbershop if he wanted a haircut. As for my first question, he said that he didn't know how to answer it. And that was where I decided we ought to leave it for now."

The female called Julian remained passive. Like her male companions, she had narrowed her vocabulary down to Yes and No. Unlike Allred Avery-McKnight and Alonso Enamorado, whose speech could occasionally be coaxed into complete sentences, the female was steadfast in her chosen monosyllables. Her father negated this, and told of instances in which he'd caught her repeating the tail end of what someone had said, particularly if she appeared to like the sound of the words. Her imitations, he'd said, could be remarkable, showing evidence of a keen ear and a good memory. He later admitted that since her homecoming, he had not partaken in a real conversation with her, one that could not be steered by Yeses and Nos.

David Livingstone spoke of a time shortly after the first early morning. It was when his daughter watched her mother make black bean soup.

Their kitchen had been redone in the years since their daughter's return. Another window had been installed and the faux-oak cabinets replaced and the linoleum ripped out and laid in adobe tiles. The refrigerator was opposite from where it had been before. The female hissed at the sound of the garbage disposal, yet displayed something that could be identified as annoyance when her mother tried to show her how to work the microwave. "And she did manage to figure it out quick enough," her mother added. "She'd never liked people telling her how to do things. She put in a Pop Tart for about fifteen seconds. It was cherry, the kinds that didn't have icing. She bit into it right away and spat it out, not because of the heat of the thing. I got it out of her that it was too sweet. It'd been awhile, I suppose, since she'd had sugar like that. And we tried not to feed our kids too much sugar growing up."

According to both parents, Julian had been a help in the kitchen. While refined sugar was used sparingly, as per the Livingstone house rule, plentiful use was made with honey, dried fruit, and fruit nectars. While not what one might recognize as a granola family, the Livingstones handed down the edict that a balanced diet made with food as fresh as you could get it was the path to a life righteously lived.

Mrs. Livingstone said, "I used to pre-soak the black beans the night before. I had her help me do that."

Now that her daughter had reappeared, Mrs. Livingstone found herself at a loss of what to do, other than feed her. Julian's favorite had been alternately called black bean stew or black bean chili. The family kept the standard ingredients on their weekly shopping lists, though now it was only the parents left in the house.

There had been two younger children, also daughters, for whom Julian had been a myth, a suggestion that the world around them was less concrete than they had thought, that, if you had wanted to, the very air might open and you could walk through to another place. Julian was not dead. They had held to this, for anything else was blasphemous. David Livingstone would not allow it, and he would have done the same, had it been Susanna or Teresa on that side of the ether.

Mrs. Livingstone thought that it might be too much, as yet, for an official family reunion. Julian had been at home for less than a day, and even the company of close relatives, her own sisters, could have made for a claustrophobic atmosphere.

In truth, Mrs. Livingstone later put in, "They wouldn't have recognized her. And she was very changed. She would've scared them."

Instead, Mrs. Livingstone chose to call her younger daughters on the phone and put the conversation on speaker. It was nearly noon. They hadn't any dried black beans, but there were cans in the pantry. There was bacon in the fridge and peppers and carrots in the crisper. Mrs. Livingstone readied the Dutch oven and diced, allowing Julian to scrape carrots.

"What she did was, she sat on the floor with the carrot between her feet, and she did it that way. I told her that she might hurt herself. She kept going as though she hadn't heard me, but she did get everything scraped clean."

What Mrs. Livingstone had amassed of her eldest daughter were two things: that she could read and write, and that her language was fluent. Her child was not wild, in the sense of never having been exposed to society and its trappings. Julian Livingstone had been what her elementary school had described as gifted, which qualified her for extracurricular enrichment that took her out of the regular school day and placed her with a small group of other students who had been labelled similarly advanced. Her parents had been pleased, initially, by this classification. In retrospect, they belittled it.

David Livingstone said, "If I remember correctly, they had them doing a lot of what you might call busy work. They learned all the phobias, triskaidekaphobia and arachnophobia and I don't know what all, and made a poster for the lobby. One time they built a trebuchet, that was kind of neat. But I think it was a solution for the school to keep the bored kids from acting out. What better way to do that than tell someone their kid is gifted?"

Mrs. Livingstone said, "She could be obstinate. She was. She was right then when we were making the stew. I think she remembered everything. How do you forget? Those first nine years are critical, I've read. You don't forget. I told her she might hurt herself, doing the carrots like that, and she ignored me. I told her she needed to sit in a chair, because she was underfoot, and she stayed on the floor. She hid under the table and pulled down the cloth when I persisted. She would pretend not to hear me before. I would get angry. But now I had no choice. I had to keep going, I couldn't get mad. Considering."

There was bacon to dice, one poblano, one yellow onion, one red bell pepper, and two carrots. Mrs. Livingstone did any knife work and Julian seemed content to watch. She would notice at certain intervals, namely those in which she had her back turned, that there was less to the bacon and vegetable piles than she'd thought. Following a mother's instinct, she peered under the kitchen table, where her daughter had squeezed herself and where she now sat munching carrot coins. There was a glow across her lips, an acrid, piggy smell in her hair.

Mrs. Livingstone sighed. "I think all I said was that if she kept eating everything on the counter, there would be less for the soup."

She had her younger daughters on the phone as she cooked, opening the three-way call with an exuberant, "Guess who's here?" At opposite ends of the line, Susanna and Teresa were firm skeptics. They could not see Julian, nor could they hear her. A debate ensued. Susanna demanded that their mother turn the call into a video chat so that she and Teresa might have proof. Their mother was unfamiliar with the various bells and whistles that her phone came with and her husband's instincts for the seemingly monthly turnover of technology were not much sharper. And anyway, he was not at home at that time. Teresa assumed the role of tech support and tried to walk her mother through the navigation of apps, the location of the camera-video function but not the video chat, restoring apps that were necessary after having deleted them by fumbling and frustration, calming her mother when it simply became too much, having been tempted to hang up when Mrs. Livingstone called her a nonbeliever and snapping in turn the question of what she thought that word was supposed to mean.

Julian repeated, "Nonbeliever."

She repeated the word many times over the course of the call.

Mrs. Livingstone told her daughter, "What an absurd thing to say." She spoke to the one on the phone as directly as the one under the table.

It became another phrase liked and picked up by Julian. "What an absurd thing to say." Her diction was clear and her accent perfect. To Mrs. Livingstone, hearing her own words so adroitly reproduced, and yet in a voice so hoarse, made her wonder if the entire incident was truly a thing of her own mind. She considered the fact that the creature under her table might not be her daughter at all. She considered also the notion that grief is a transcendent experience, continuing in hills and valleys, alternately accepting and gnashing one's teeth at the loss from one year to the next, and then years as decades. It was conceivable to believe that in that time, she might have lost her mind. Perhaps she had conjured the entire homecoming. There was no grave, but the memorial bench was firmly in place. She had only her husband to vouch for it.

"And who were they to say?" Mrs. Livingstone later said, with some venom. "Suzy and Terri weren't here when she came back. They hadn't seen her yet. And I think for once they were glad I couldn't figure out this damn phone because I don't think they wanted to have her back. Not that they didn't love their sister. I believe they did. But they were so young when it happened. Maybe everything makes more sense from the perspective of two people, instead of three. Maybe it's more convenient to think of her as some cautionary tale. Caution against what, I don't know. I think, more than anything, they wanted to be right about this."

The call ended with sighs and sour pacifisms and apologies. Susanna and Teresa agreed to attend a small party that weekend at their parents' house. It would be a cookout.

When Mrs. Livingstone let the black bean stew simmer, she went out to the backyard to survey the garden's weed situation and to see if anything needed to be pruned before the gathering. She harbored faith and entertained visions of a true family reunion that would and should occur on that very spot, right where she stood. Though unwilling to make an outright confession of it, she had often been seduced by the idea of "If you can dream it, you can be it" and sometimes took that sentiment a little farther, with the notion in mind that if you could dream it clearly enough, then what you were envisioning was not a montage of wishful thinking but a projection into your very future.

She later admitted that, in part, she had wanted to get away from Julian, whose repetitions put her teeth on edge. Mrs. Livingstone explained that they were not completely unfamiliar to her, as her eldest had been a keen mimic and would often do impressions of the people she knew, teachers, the school bus driver, children in her class. These imitations were spot-on, often reciting verbatim things she had heard her subject say, often things they would rather not have said themselves, often shocked and often offended that the child who had been standing around or mooning around them had paid their monologue any attention.

David Livingstone said, "It was how one of her gifted teachers got herself fired, actually. I won't repeat, but Jule happened to be in the room when certain things were said. I guess she'd forgotten about her. And, lo and behold, I get home from work and she's making her sisters roar with laughter. This particular teacher had a kind of funny way of gesturing and she wore a lot of rings. That was what set Suzy and Terri off. Jule had put the sterling silver napkin rings on her fingers and put some raspberries on her fingertips, because this teacher also had bright red nails. And I knew Jule was telling the truth because none of these impressions were ever really off the cuff. She was like a recording device."

Mrs. Livingstone said, "She could sometimes be cruel about it. I had to tell her to stop making fun of the handicapped kids in the other class. I had to tell her she was lucky that she had what she had. Therefore, the grace of God—" She stopped. "You didn't want to be the butt of one of her jokes."

Satisfied with the state of the garden, Mrs. Livingstone turned to go back in. She had worried that, while she was outside, something might have happened in the kitchen. For example, that something might burn, something might spill, something might smash to bits on the adobe tile floor. She had not expected to worry that her eldest might follow her outside, which she had. Her eldest, in a sudden bowel upset, had left an intermittent trail from just inside the kitchen door, across the porch, to the shed, behind which she now squatted. Her mother watched, more fascinated than mortified, as her eldest dug into the ground with her hands and buried of her waste what she could.

Mrs. Livingstone said, "She looked at me and called me a nonbeliever. I think she meant it."

When further questioned about their spiritual beliefs, the Enamorados stated again that they were conscientious objectors. Alonso's father had been jailed in his youth for avoiding the draft and had his record expunged when pacifism became a larger voice in the popular language of the day. He and his wife led their family in prayer before meals but amended that exclude those taken in restaurants, as they viewed public prayer as ostentatious and disingenuous. They did not advocate martial arts outside of practices made to disarm only; they had allowed their sons to take aikido in the summers. They prohibited the entry of many films into the home, banning *The Breakfast Club* for its lack of respect toward women; Marisol used for example a scene in which Judd Nelson, head trapped between Molly Ringwald's thighs, gawps at her panties under a table.

"We didn't want him growing up with those images in his head," she said. "They stay with you."

Alonso's father put in that his own father had been a carouser whose antics, despite an intimidating business presence, had left the family devastated, and as adulthood approached, he had determined what kind of man he wanted to be. He knew a man to be what his father was not. "A man comes home to his wife every night," he said, "A man provides for his children. A man uses his words. A man uses his heart to inform the mind, not the other way around. A man does not raise his fist in retaliation."

Donna McKnight began an archeological dig of sorts in her basement. She had wanted to find evidence of the boy whom she had lost that might reconcile with the creature in his place. This was her word, as confessed. The creature, who had by now been to a doctor, a barber, a Kohl's, a Target, and a TJ Maxx, in addition to the maze of aisles that made up the various supermarkets in the area. She acknowledged that he looked like her son. She recognized features, apart from the eye with its dilated pupil, that recalled her father or an aunt or a grandfather. Unbeknownst to Allred and to her husband, she had taken a parentage test, just to be sure, and their relation was confirmed by ninety-nine-point-nine percent. There was no room for doubt.

Her son, as a child, had been a good listener, an active participant, a problem solver, a creative thinker, a pleasure to have in class, so said the report cards and progress reports unearthed in a box from OfficeMax marked AL. An assessment from nursery school recommended a smaller class size for him, due to a tendency to disrupt, to talk out of turn, to interrupt. Following the assessment, she had looked into the private day school in their neighborhood, taken interviews, prepped her son for the entrance exam, and enrolled him with the intention of continuing his education there from kindergarten through sixth grade.

He had been strong in mathematics. He had experienced some difficulty spelling, and Joel would review vocabulary words with him every night after dinner so that Al would be ready for the test at the end of each week. There were school bluebooks, lined and filled with columns in blocky letters that showed his progress, having spelled *receipt* with an IE and writing it out fifty times until he spelled it with an EI. In a joint project with his art class, his third grade teacher had supervised the children in the making of their own individual sticker books, made from sheets of wax paper with covers cut to size from wallpaper samples and stapled together. Behold rows of stars and green alien faces and Valentine's hearts and affirmations, GREAT! and SUPER!!! and KEEP IT UP! Ten stickers awarded you a prize on Fridays from a grab bag: a new pencil, an eraser in the shape of an animal or a pink brain or a puffy yellow hand in the thumb's up gesture. Twenty bought you one free ice cream bar and slice of pizza on Pizza Days, which fell on Thursdays on a biweekly schedule. At fifty stickers, you were allowed to name the amphibians in the class terrarium and to take one frog home to look after for the weekend. Allred had named his frog Phil. "For Phil Collins," his mother had laughed. "We'd sing songs from *The Way We Walk* album. We sang a lot on the way to school a lot that year."

Noting that Al had a talent for singing, his parents enrolled him in a summer theater program for children ages eight to twelve. It had a reputation for its rigor and there was a lengthy audition process. Parents and teachers alike affirmed its professional atmosphere, with some boasting that it had inspired several ingenues to seek agents, to see if this could be a stepping-stone toward work in television commercials or perhaps a spot in a real theater production or a movie.

Donna Avery McKnight found the playbill wedged in between the wax paper pages of the sticker book. The show had taken place the summer before Al vanished, with two evening performances and a Sunday matinee. It was a song-and-dance revue of works inspired by choreographer Bob Fosse, chintzily titled, *Fosse Kidz.* The lineup was:

"Magic to Do"
"All That Jazz"
"Razzle Dazzle"
"Dancin' Man"
"On Broadway"
"Who's Got the Pain?"
"Steam Heat"
"Sing Sing Sing"
"Everything Old is New Again"
"Bye Bye Blackbird"

Donna Avery McKnight had penciled stars next to the numbers her son would be in: "Magic to Do", "Dancin' Man", "On Broadway", "Everything Old is New Again", and "Bye Bye Blackbird". from the bottom of the box, she pulled the CD that Joel had burned of all ten songs, ripped from their respective soundtracks, so that Al would be prepared.

"And he was," Joel and Donna McKnight said. "He

was great. He seemed to love it."

When asked about friendships made within the theater group, Donna McKnight could not recollect any new bonds or acquaintances. "From what I know, Al stuck to his usual crew. He could be exuberant on the stage, but he was what you might call a shy guy. We had to nudge him to make new friends." She gave the names of four children in his class and two in the class ahead whose birthday parties he had attended, in whose homes he had spent the night. None of them were those with whom he had left civilization for a life in the woods.

"That was what he called it," Joel McKnight added. "No location. The woods."

Donna McKnight had taken a closer look at the playbill for *Fosse Kidz*. Yes, she knew that the program had attracted children from around the area, from many different schools. She bristled when pressed further about the participation of certain others. The McKnights lived off Natural Spring Road, which is in close proximity to Tarsus Road and Lower Albert Road. They recognized photographs of the boy Evander and the girl Clare, and repeated with some fervor that their son had had no previous interaction with them or with the girl Mary Kathleen, who, for reasons unknown, had not attended the public, private day, or parochial school as the other children had, and was instead homeschooled by her mother.

Nevertheless, it gave Donna McKnight cause to

review the cast list one more time and take better notice of who had done which numbers. The boy Evander and the girls Clare and Mary Kathleen had danced in "Magic to Do", "Dancin' Man", "On Broadway", "Everything Old is New Again", and "Bye Bye Blackbird".

She said, "He never brought them over. He never talked about them. He never mentioned them."

Marisol Enamorado and her husband thought it best to allow some time to pass before approaching the families of the boy Evander and the girls Clare and Mary Kathleen. At this juncture, few knew of her son's return, as few knew of the girl Julian and the boy Allred. Like the Livingstones and the McKnights, the Enamorados had wanted to keep what they felt to be a miracle for themselves for as long as they could hold out. Of course, in time, an announcement would have to be made. They had prolonged despair these two decades, and only last year had they given in to what they were prepared to call the "reality of the situation" and declared their son legally dead. A kernel of faith prevented them from purchasing a headstone and, as Marisol Enamorado testified, prayers for Alonso's return continued, though they were no longer spoken aloud at the dinner table. These requests devolved to covert, silent codes, for the majesty of proper liturgy seemed more and more like the trappings of a mawkish drama. It occurred to the family that people, while sympathetic, while helpful, had placed a measured distance between themselves and the Enamorados. Marisol wondered at first if it was superstition, that by association, whatever had whisked away Alonso would come for their children, too, like the boogeyman. When she realized how silly that was, she approached it the matter again, this time with a new suspicion, one that seemed to fit: That, tainted by tragedy, the Enamorados had become fascinating. They had become fiction. People peered in, if not through their windows, then through whispers. They had become a cautionary tale—but this Marisol Enamorado quickly dismissed upon observing the lack of change in the usual neighborhood routines, that children continued to walk to school and troll the cul-de-sacs alone. No petitions circulated. No neighborhood watch was installed. No one drove their kids to school unless they had to. They had become fiction, this was true, as Alonso became the boy who had vanished. This time, the boogeyman was not to blame, but an alien abduction or a rapture. These musings, fantastic as they were, implied a willfulness on the part of the one who had gone. The Enamorados were good people. No one quite wanted to broach the possibility that their son had simply run away.

Because what had there been to run away from? This was Marisol Enamorado's question. "When you're that small, where can you go? How do you live? You have no idea. You might think about it, and maybe you'll even set a course and start out, but sooner or later, you turn around and come right back home." This conjecture came from her own experience, when, as a small girl of about seven or eight and following an unjust sentence of going to bed without supper, Marisol crept out of her first-floor bedroom window and walked out into the night with the hazy plan of living in the park around the corner until her parents sought her out and apologized. She contemplated sleeping on the tennis court and living off what she could forage from the trash cans, and these things were enough to make her turn around when she reached the end of her driveway. Her parents were none the wiser for her act of rebellion.

When asked if anything had called her to leave her bedroom, Marisol was firm that nothing had. "It was very much an *I'll-show-you* mentality. You know. I'll show you, Mom and Dad, for sending me to bed without supper and being so mean. It came completely from within."

Meanwhile, Alonso was adapting to the old home with the aloofness of a guest. As it had been the first morning, he did not move to be touched and would stiffen when touched. Toward affection, he was distrustful but willing, in the manner of a foreigner adapting to a new culture. Clothes and shoes he wore with some resentment, though he understood that clothes and shoes were the custom of this house, these people. At first, he would consume only water and raw vegetables, and seemed wary of packaged food. As for meat, his mother might have said early on that he turned up his nose, under the assumption that it repulsed him, later amending that he appeared frightened by it and that in turning away from it, he would not be in violation of any rule or law. He waited for an invitation to sit with the family at mealtimes, and he waited for his turn to speak. Like the girl Julian, his voice was hoarse and could not project at a certain pitch, as per tones in normal conversation. He could, however, when needed, raise his voice in a high, clear whoop that could be heard for miles around. It rose from the chest and burst from him, not quite a caw and not quite an ape's hooting. This was discovered on a day when his father put the car into drive instead of reverse and had nearly barreled through the garage and into the backyard. Marisol admitted that her husband, in recent years, had grown more and more forgetful, and she suspected that this change was upsetting to her son.

"It's little things," she said. "He remembers Alonso, of course. But it's little things like words, where things are, how you work this and that. He was Mr. Can Do. He knew something about everything. He taught calculus. He was a deacon and he did the accounting for our church. He's an old man. I don't know if that's something Alonso ever thought about while he was away."

When asked if she meant Alonso's father becoming an old man, she shook her head. She hesitated to speculate more on her son's time away. She referred to Alonso as he had been before and as he was now. He had vanished at nine and reappeared at thirty. The years in between seemed untouchable, as yet, to her.

There was a lapse, a silence, that was soon broken by Marisol, a sound that was not quite a bark and not quite a laugh. The situation did not yield for much humor, but with a smile, she said, "I used to wish that I could just skip certain parts of life. Just skip ahead to the next decade. I used to make that wish when I was in grammar school and when I was in junior high and when I was in high school. I would say, If only I could just skip all this and be thirty and be done with it."

Then, just as quick, the humor has quit the room. From this new place, as if from the bottom of a pit, Marisol asked, "I'll tell you what. I never expected him to go around this house, looking in room to room, and asking in that voice if we were going to kill him."

Julian, according to her father, was willing to share some of what her time away had been like.

In concert with Marisol Enamorado and the McKnight families, David Livingstone understood that his daughter had lived in the woods. There was no further description, no precise location. "The woods," were her words. In the woods, there had been rules. In

Julian's words, there had been customs. David Livingstone reported her having said of this or that as being or not being the custom. There had been things which one did and did not do.

He recalled, "I read *The Secret Garden* with her not too long before she went. I believe that was where she picked up that language of something being the custom. Because at the start of the book, when the little girl is just off the boat from India, everything to her is or is not the custom."

He had read it to her again since her homecoming. They went about it as they had when she was small, wherein, he would read and she would repeat, syllable by syllable, sounding each word out until she could read the page herself with fluency. By nine, the slow sounding out had relegated itself to the lengthy or the outright foreign. Now, at thirty, David Livingstone found it difficult to determine whether or not hope could be mined from the situation, whether he should mourn his daughter's apparently devolved literacy or to rejoice in her ability to remember simple words. She had written out those addresses, after all.

When asked why the Livingstone family had waited for as long as they had to inform the parents, all of whom at the time still lived at the addresses, David Livingstone continued as though the subject had not changed.

As for regular communication, these reveries

were rare and brief. Julian's preferred method of echoing mimicry largely prevailed, though her ability to talk about what had happened during those missing years did not indicate a real willingness on her part, so thought her father.

"It looked to me as though she were waiting for permission to say more," he said. "She would pause. She would look away, kind of over one shoulder, and then she would go on, albeit with hesitation. And then, when she felt we were pressing too much, she would clam up, and it might be days before anyone could get her talking again. Well, outside of the repeating-echoing."

It was from these snatched bits of clarity among his daughter's woolgathering that David Livingstone was able to put together a rough idea of how his daughter had lived into a notebook, a Deuteronomic list accompanied by his own observations and speculations which he titled *Rules for Living in the Woods*. According to his daughter, these were:

Thou shalt not kill.

Do no harm.

The first two edicts, David Livingstone noted, appeared to be of particular importance to this small society, and he amended the list to illustrate their separation from the rest by putting them in capitals and underlining them. He said that it was of particular importance to him and to his family that these were two key rules lived by his daughter. It was of particular importance to him because he had taught them to her. Like the Emanorados, the Livingstones belonged to a similar branch of faith that prioritized an intellectual approach to conflict. David Livingstone found religion not long after his retirement from the Marines and the subsequent birth of his first child. He feinted at having seen things in the field and refused to elaborate. In his girls' upbringing, he and his wife refrained from spanking and resorted instead to "very stern talking-tos" or a chore along the lines of vacuuming the upstairs bedrooms or weeding the flowerbeds. Like the Enamorados, the Livingstone girls were encouraged to bank any kindling flame of anger. David Livingstone repurposed a cleaned-out peanut butter jar and installed it in the kitchen by the microwave as a curse jar, a dollar for four letter words, two dollars when anyone took the Lord's name in vain. When the jar was full, the family would go out to Mamacita's for dinner.

Did the Livingstones know the Enamorados? Or had they?

From this, a steely eye and a strict, "No."

The Enamorados were of a similar faith, but not the same. Their houses of worship were at the opposite ends of town. Their children had gone to different schools. David Livingstone conceded that while it was possible, it was very unlikely that their paths would have crossed.

Thou shalt not kill.

Do no harm.

The first was the sixth out of the Ten Commandments.

The second came from the Hippocratic oath which doctors take upon completing medical school. The modern version reads, "I will remember that I remain a member of society, with special obligations to all my fellow human beings." Its earliest inception, translated from the Koine Greek, reads, "I swear by Apollo Healer, by Asclepius, by Hygieia, by Panacea, and by all the gods and goddesses, making them my witnesses, that I will carry out, according to my ability and judgment, this oath and this indenture."

David Livingstone said of Julian, "She went through a phase for about a year before she went where she wanted to be a doctor. The year before that, her goal in life was to be an airborne ranger. And before that, maybe from about four to six, she wanted to be a garbage collector, then an architect, then a movie director, then an electrician. I don't know how much stock to put into any of that. She would get worked up about it for a while and kind of go through the motions, learn all the lingo, and then drop it for something else. It was closer to stepping into a role, like an actor would. Once she'd dropped it, she'd forget everything about being an airborne ranger or whatever it was."

A photograph offered a creature that was not beautiful, however possessive of an aristocratic allure, aloof, as though looking out over a nation newly colonized and newly hers. She did not quite smile for the camera. Her hair was combed and French-braided and cut with bangs in the front, the braid over one shoulder. In her countenance was impatience, arrogance, a tightness around the jaw suggesting a covert gritting of teeth for having to sit still.

By present comparison, in a photo documenting the cookout, here was the same creature, clothed in a t-shirt and a long, tiered skirt, her hair loose around her shoulders, electrified by the heat, with bangs again to create a semblance of shape. The excess hair that had grown along her back and flanks and neck and between her breasts had fallen away, now that she no longer needed it. Her arms were ropy and serviceable as an extra pair of legs. Her hands were callused at the knuckles, but these were largely hidden by her stance for the picture, in the fig leaf pose, folded over her groin. Still impatient, still arrogant, still grinding her teeth behind a mouth that was straight, save for a token upturn at one corner. If anything, she was taller.

As for the rules following, they were:

No speech.

No sex.

No things.

No clothes.

When asked by her father to elaborate on the reasonings behind these edicts, Julian was silent, save for her stern repetition of them, as if to further drive home their meaning.

No speech.

No sex.

No things.

No clothes.

David Livingstone allowed for a private moment of contrition, as his daughter had kept to (he liked to think) as true to this code as possible. Whereas, not even he had honored the Decalogue in its fullness.

"It shouldn't be so difficult," he murmured. "But it's very deceptive."

"These are the customs," as Julian had said.

Pam Jones

They Acclimate

Alonso Enamorado spent much of his time, as per his mother's testimony, going from room to room, shuttling from one furtive glance to another, asking these people who had fulfilled and vowed to go on fulfilling that sacred oath to protect, feed, clothe, and love him without condition if they were going to kill him.

His father was aghast. "I'd never touch a hair on his head."

Alonso Enamorado had never been spanked as a child. He had never known violence. He had never known depravity. Nor had he known neglect. His parents took him to the barber, the Kohl's, the family GP, and to the church elders he had been ministered to as a boy. His hair was no longer serviceably wooly and he was clean shaven. He took many warm showers, in spite of the heat and the public reminders to conserve water. Like his companions at opposite ends of the neighborhood sprawl, the downy, dark fur that had accumulated over the years along his back and shoulders and arms and legs and neck began to fall out, first in stringy morsels, then in handfuls. His mother pulled them up from the drain using a coat hanger and abrasive chemicals from the S.C. Johnson Company.

It was understood by everyone in the household that Alonso's usual method of walking, that is, his accustomed gait that made use of all four limbs along the ground and made extra feet out of his hands, would not be tolerated. He was able to change stances quickly enough when prompted, from quadruped to homo erectus, responding as though to an electrical shock when his mother or father directed him, as they had when their son slumped at the table at seven or eight or nine, to "Straighten up."

Now and then, to these nudges, he would croak, "Are you going to kill me?"

He became covetous of clothes and preferred items with pockets. Many of the shirts his mother bought at Kohl's were of the button-up variety with a pocket in the front, as were the t-shirts. Once dressed, he recalled and realized the cache potential of pockets, and so it came to pass that his mother would notice a disappearance of small items, keys, mechanical pencils, paper clips, thumbtacks, the slim, snaky charging cables for phones that were coiled at this or that end of the house and come to trace these things in the bulges forming at her son's chest or hips. When his mother asked, her son complied, without explanation, and while his pockets remained empty, the treasure trove simply reappeared, now secured in the toes of his boyhood shoes at the back of his closet, found when his mother was gathering laundry.

When asked if anyone in the family had exhibited a hoarding tendency, Marisol described a cousin who, newly returned from overseas, took to bringing canned goods and bottled water into his bedroom and storing his provisions under the bed. The cousin had come to live with them when his own mother, perplexed at the change in her own son, could no longer cope, just as he could no longer cope. He did not touch the canned goods and the bottled water. He did not sleep through the night, nor did he sleep during the day. He had seen combat, but his mother was certain that this behavior and that ordeal were unrelated. He spoke very little of it, save for his mother's punctuation that he heard voices and had experienced a lapse of time and place. In his words, as per his memory, which was undamaged, he was called away from his peers and told to leave his belongings where they were. Further instructions were that he remove his shoes, for he would not need them where he was going. His commanding officer reported him missing when all that remained of him at his post were his folded uniform, his helmet, his weapon, his boots. His commanding officer reported his recovery five days later, in a portion of the desert that was the farthest from any point of civilization or water. The cousin was hydrated and nourished, despite his location, naked but unharmed, untouched but altered. He refused to address his commanding officer or anyone else. He counted and recounted the currency on his person and developed a habit of checking his debit account multiple times in an hour. He did not fulfill his assigned tasks and did not speak to his former comrades and compatriots, all of whom had previously described the individual as easygoing, affable, a good soldier, a good guy, nothing special, nothing strange.

Marisol hesitated before allowing that her cousin had claimed, in that time, to have spoken with God. A psychiatric evaluation countered this with a shifting diagnosis, schizophrenic or schizotypal or schizoaffective. As a child, she had been a skeptic, though the mistrust had not been in her maker but in, what she then felt and dreamed and understood to be, lies from her very species. At seven or eight or nine, however old she had been when her cousin came to live in their guest bedroom, Marisol had kept a finely tuned ear to all things she perceived as stories, fairy tales, or general grown-up untruths. She had wanted to meet someone who made contact with the one, true Lord for as long as she could remember, and took it with a grain of salt when her mother told her in the privacy of a car ride to the Dairy Queen that her cousin was crazy. She had been largely kept away from him, with the exception of mealtimes, which with him, were infrequent. She caught him a few times eating a raw onion like an apple, whole and in big bites, before someone would come along and tell her to leave her cousin alone.

Once and only once had she secured a private moment with him, and peppered him with questions. What did God look like? Was the Lord a he or sometimes a she? Why had her cousin been told to remove his shoes? Why had he taken nothing with him when he went into the driest part of the desert? What did God sound like?

To these inquiries, her cousin had said:

God was amorphous, but had appeared to him in a dream as a great ape.

God was amorphous, therefore genderless.

Without his shoes, his feet would become longer, as they were meant to be.

In the desert—this was where her faith grew shaky—in the desert, you can't remember your name, and there ain't no one for to give you no pain.

"America," she said, then clarified, "They did that song that goes, *I been through the desert on a horse with no name.*"

Allred McKnight distressed at the appearance of his feet. He had been to the general practitioner several times more, where it was first noted that, while the toes were not quite webbed, their marked distance from each other, particularly the big toe from the four smaller ones, as well as a low heel, gave the impression that the overall structure belonged to a creature quite apart from his own species. The patient was as inclined to use his feet as his hands, as grabbing instruments, and his lower set of appendages proved to be as dexterous as those above, capable of peeling an orange or folding a piece of paper into precise accordion pleats. In the weeks following his homecoming, however, the midsections of both feet had begun to stiffen, causing Allred to complain of severe cramps. There was a brief interlude, of about forty-eight hours, in which the patient was unable to walk for the pain. A visit to the emergency room revealed no broken bones or sprains, save for what the observing doctor thought to be a series of charley horses. To him and in his words, he pronounced both feet to be in fine fettle. Here was where the patient wept. The change had happened first in a succession of increments, of skin tightening, which were such that the patient could easily ignore the symptoms of, what he strongly felt to be, his devolution. This latest had seemingly occurred overnight: An expansion of the heel and, being now a greater source of pain than his feet's midsections, an upward migration the big toe from its previous location around the ball of the foot to rejoin the four small toes at the top. It was the picture of a healthy human foot. The patient was revolted by it.

Paul, the general practitioner, asked him at their next appointment why he thought his feet were now hideous.

At this point, the pain had been dealt with by administration of Benadryl and the worst was over. The patient was again ambulatory, though his gait had become hesitant. He moved in slow, shuffling steps, and said that he could no longer keep his balance. Up to now, the patient had been let to go barefoot to the general practitioner's office, as no shoes would fit; as prehensile appendages, the feet could not hold them, either causing frustration at having to negotiate the thumblike big toes or slipping out of them completely due to the low, flat heels. This day, he sported the Converse high tops.

The general practitioner asked the patient how his shoes felt.

The patient worried that because his feet felt very hot and moist inside them, that they were now ripe for infection. His mother was now enforcing the donning of socks, too.

"She wants you to wear socks anytime you wear shoes?" the general practitioner pressed.

The patient clarified, adding that his mother wanted him to get used to wearing socks and shoes and introduced a regime to instill the importance of a daily routine, starting with getting dressed. She laid out new things she purchased from Kohl's or Penney's or Target on his desk chair, as she'd done before his disappearance. They would sit in a pyramid until morning, with jeans and t-shirt topped off by underpants and socks, and a sweatshirt or flannel draped over the back of the chair in case of a chill. At seven-thirty, his mother or stepfather would knock and enter and watch to make sure he put everything on.

The general practitioner nodded. "And how does everything else feel?" This in reference to the patient's shirt and jeans.

The patient said that he did not experience temperature in the way that everyone else seemed to, and was therefore hot and itchy at first. He conceded that his mother had started using a different brand of detergent and also throwing softener sheets into the dryer, and that this had helped somewhat. He stated, however, that he was confused at his parents' persistence, despite their witnessing his plain discomfort, and went on to say that it was not his custom to do anything that might cause himself or anyone else discomfort.

The general practitioner explained that the discomfort he was experiencing was really very minor and that it was simply a matter of getting used to things like this again. He said also that it would certainly cause many people a great deal of discomfort if the patient were to, say, enter a supermarket unclothed. People might be frightened.

The patient asked why that would be, and elaborated that the people in this scenario would see that he was unarmed.

The female known as Julian Livingstone said that the sojourn away was driven by God. This her father did not believe. He did not believe it because he had heard the phrase before, in relation to what was on high. He had heard it on AM radio and among certain of other believers as code for a loved one that had strayed from the narrow path but was sure to be brought back in the manner of the prodigal son. The loved ones were addicted to meth or crack or smack. They were homosexual or something like it. They were in danger of losing their faith and their sojourn away was necessary in order to make the return, garner forgiveness.

It had grated on him then. To him, it rendered useless the time spent eschewing vice altogether. He'd sown his wild oats, he was the first to admit it. But it was quite another thing to make mischief and expect forgiveness.

Folks at his place of worship began referring to this or that wayward relative as having sojourned. Not to worry; it was driven by God. He'd half expected someone to call his daughter's disappearance a sojourn when it happened, and, thankfully, no one dared. In two separate moments of absolute spite, somewhere in the first weeks of going into his eldest daughter's bedroom in the morning to wake her for school and finding it empty and somewhere in the days following her homecoming, again finding his daughter's bed empty but locating her via a trail of thin, sour drips around the house, the days before they thought to diaper her, as the McKnights had their son, he'd wanted to ask the mouthers of this slogan if any of the sojourners ever came back.

He wanted, too, to ask them if they knew what he knew. "About her," he said of Julian, and added, "About myself."

In the attitude of one who is unsure if the events he recounts are nothing at all or the tip of catastrophe, with sighs and pauses, David Livingstone described a memory. Actually, they were two incidents, separated by decades. However, Julian's father said, it was important to think of the incident as singular, yet from two opposing perspectives. He sighed again. He almost scoffed. "I'm not sure if this means anything."

When he was in elementary school, his parents moved the family from the state capitol to a small town, where they were partway through building the house that they would live in. "In the meantime, we had two trailers set up around the foundation and all the construction activity, and for maybe four or five months, we hunkered down there." He recalled at seven or eight going up to the unfinished second floor. The new house was to be a large one, to accommodate a growing family, of which David Livingstone would be the eldest of five children. Of the bare second floor, he said, "You went up a flight of stairs that was already carpeted and then you were up and out again. It was all scaffolding, nothing but the bare-bones structure. You know, all that raw wood." They reminded him of pillars in a temple. "You had to be careful of how close to the edge you got. My folks didn't like me going up there for fear of falling." But who should be up there, among the wooden pillars, with his toes over the edge's lip? "My father was standing in the area that became the upstairs bathroom. Not the master bath. This was the one that I used and my sisters and brother used for the twenty-five-odd years we had that house." With his toes over the edge's lip, the elder Livingstone gently placed more of his weight on the balls of his feet. He would hesitate, letting his heels stagger backward so that his feet were flat. A moment would pass, wherein, he appeared to his son to have turned to stone, very still and turned blankly out over the panoramic view that was his empire, the property, the acreage, the manor. And he would let his toes take the weight again.

"And I thought," David Livingstone allowed, "it wouldn't take very much to give him one good shove, would it? God forgive me, but that's what I did."

The elder Livingstone landed in the bed of one of the pickup trucks that were parked in a ring around the foundation. He landed in a way that shielded him from much more than a bruised tailbone. He maintained unto his death that he had experienced a moment of dizziness and blamed the day's heat and dehydration.

The younger shook his head. "I'm certain he knew it was me."

When pressed, the younger, with eyes shut and breath fast, as though he were hauling the foulest sulfur from a toxic mine, he hissed, "When you are punished without reason, and you continue to be punished, you're almost being dared to do the thing you're accused of, aren't you? How could I look at it any other way? I mean. I mean, come on. Julian did the exact same thing when we built this place."

The same incident, decades removed.

When she was in kindergarten, David Livingstone moved the family from the small town to the state capitol, where they were partway through building the house in which they now lived. He, his wife and his daughter hunkered down in their own trailer at an RV park for four or five months until the house's completion.

David Livingstone was tempted to say that it was because children were another species entirely from their eventual, matured form. "They know right from wrong, but not cause and effect. In adulthood, you learn by having observed customs and conventions. You imitate. And the imitation, one day, sticks." He paused. "I can't speak for anyone else, I suppose. I can attest to the fact that I took the phrase, Fake it 'til you make it, very much to heart."

When asked to elaborate, David Livingstone recounted a celebrity interview of a pop star who described having to interact with and cater to shifting whorls of stadium fans each night as having to put on her human suit. It conjured in his mind the image of a chimpanzee, huffing and knuckle-dragging through a closet until it found the garment, rough to the touch, chameleonically odorous, but necessary, and easy enough to get in and out of because it had a zipper in the back. Once you wrestled into it, your posture straightened. Your feet changed. You no longer smelled the way you did and therefore, you were not as easily recognized. You no longer detected the smells of others and lost the salience of what those smells meant. You knew that you could not determine intent based alone on the patterns of facial movement, which were both solid and quicksilver.

"But you learn all that, don't you?"

Asked what any of that might have done to warrant a sojourn away with God, David Livingstone posed a question of his own. He said, "Because if that was the case, why couldn't I have been whisked away, too? The Lord is not Peter Pan."

Asked what occurred at the other end of this incident, David Livingstone recalled having stepped out of the way in time. He recalled having stepped out of the way in time and of his daughter, small, singular, fierce, charging over the unguarded second story edge, his own hand appearing within his frame of focus and snatching her braid, again in time. Asked what he thought in that moment in which he held his daughter by her braid, he allowed that it wouldn't have taken very much to just drop her.

He looked up. "Would it? But I didn't."

"Are you going to kill me?" their son asked for the hundredth or perhaps two hundredth time.

Alonso had been playing *Myst*, or, he had been observing as his father walked him through the gameplay. There were no real villains in the series, no sudden noises, no violence. You, the player, collected clues, unveiled cyphers, operated machinery, solved puzzles.

He had been attending church where pacifists gathered. To Marisol and her husband's knowledge, there were no villains here, either; they had all reformed, and none of their sins were unpardonable. There was no talk of damnation. Hell as a place of torment was considered an unbiblical interpretation, also blasphemous, to view their Maker as a petty God prone to tantrums.

He sat behind his father's ergonomic swivel chair and in the metal folding chairs on Sundays, at first hulking, furred, heavy-browed, unsmiling, wary. Folks greeted him warmly, if from a distance of a few feet.

They remembered him and he did not remember them. They, from that width of three or so feet in the parking lot of the Masonic Lodge where the Sabbath was conducted, recounted stories of Alonso's boyhood as bright tales, collected and bound in an anthology of a life that he himself could not recall. The tellers of these tales addressed him directly, placing him at a place or time or event, calling him "You". You were just this high when you helped Sister Nancy serve at Easter. You made the best Angel Gabriel in the nativity play. You were so helpful when you pulled Aleah's baby tooth, how scared she was, how you talked to her about her favorite movie so she wouldn't have to think about it when it happened.

Aleah, from a distance of ten feet, close to her car, waved. Her smile was closed and tight.

Alonso, despite the direct address, could not reconcile the title of "You" with the hero of these tales. Because memory failed to trigger these events and because no one used his name, he thought of You as a fictional character, and was displeased. Not out of fear of slander, nor insult. He did not recall, and so it must be a lie—a flattering one, but a lie, nonetheless.

He said to Marisol, following one Sunday service, "Tell everyone to stop telling stories about me."

By then, he had shrunk. His shoulders did not stoop as much, and in time, he stood nearly erect. His parents, otherwise baffled by the situation, decided to take this as an encouraging sign, one of acclamation.

Like Allred McKnight, Alonso Enamorado's feet began the process of metamorphosis, the toes coming together to appear less and less like hands by the day. Unlike his counterpart, he did not, according to his parents, experience any discomfort during the change, or he did not appear to.

"But," Marisol put in, "he wasn't the kind of kid who would tell you if something hurt. He'd sprained his ankle pretty badly once on a Scout trip. He hiked a mile and a half on it. He was half-blind from the pain, I'm sure."

In an effort to reintroduce his son to his old life, Alonso's father brought out the photo albums. The idea was to sift through the volumes documenting Alonso's life from birth to the time just prior to his disappearance. He sat blankly through the turning of pages, of spreading overstuffed tomes to share across his lap and his father's, to identify imagery of an anonymous pink sphere probing out of baby blue swaddling. Sometimes his father would confuse the photographs, for the albums were not shelved in order, and a grinning imp at the foot of a Christmas tree or a three-foot tall pumpkin with arms and legs and moony face smeared with melted Halloween candy could be interchangeable as father for son, despite the quality of the photograph. As for Alonso, when asked if he remembered this or that holiday, he would nod, passive, despite the neat hand that had inscribed the date below each photo, whether it read

"X-mas, 1960" or "August, last day of Scout camp, 1999".

It was when his father opened an album documenting his own youth spent on a commune that Alonso showed interest. His parents had been, if not outright hippies, freethinkers disenchanted by the societal norm, though they did wear beads and paisley. They had lived on a farm without running water or electricity, and there was only one vehicle, principally used to ferry one member or another into town to use the drugstore's pay phone. Everyone shared a large old house and prayed together at mealtimes. They grew their own vegetables, Marisol said, and added, cheekily, "Plus our own grass."

Alonso wanted to know what their rules were.

Both mother and father found themselves somewhat taken aback by the question. Of course, the commune had rules. The severity of his tone made them laugh. The severity of his look made them stop. They gathered themselves and explained that, while there was no ironclad decree, outside of the Ten Commandments, community members were expected to share what they had and to be respectful and mindful of one another. There were several families there, this was true, the idea being that they lived as one under God.

Alonso pointed to certain pictures featuring these families. Some were standard issue, a husband and a wife haloed by a radiant brood. Some showed a single husband, flanked by a bevvy of wives, their children fanned behind them and stacked like a choir. He asked his father if he'd had other wives, as well. To this, his father somewhat shamefaced in the eyes of his present wife, Alonso's parents told him about Margaret and turned the page in search of a woman with blondish hair plaited over one shoulder. It was the only photograph they had of her alone. Alonso's father said that the second marriage was not a legal one, but a spiritual union, as per the way of the commune. The arrangement was short-lived, and further photographs documented her severance from the Enamorados and eventual absorption by another man's harem.

The group split halfway through the Reagan administration, with many of the factions regrouping to form the church the family attended, just preceding the birth of their only son to the present.

"It wasn't something that came naturally to either of us," Marisol would later say. "We'd been together since college. The expectation was to populate the earth with good stewards. It was the seventies. We were idealistic. We thought we could switch off anything as petty as insecurity. He couldn't perform." She stopped, shocked at her admission, her bluntness. "He couldn't do it. Not with her. Not anybody else, and there were offers. I'm glad now that he couldn't—with Margaret. At the time, I actually feared for the welfare of the planet, that the tide would rush in or the bomb would drop or the meteor would hit—I don't know—and that our population would be less a few good stewards when the earth was scraped clean."

Their one son, having heard the same, wanted to know what had kept his father from performing with anyone else.

To which, his parents answered that God intended marriage to be for two people, consenting adults who were as committed to each other as the Redeemer to his ministry.

Alonso asked who the Redeemer was and was told. His parents' church did not have imagery to offer, as their faith prevented icons and shrines of any kind. It was idolatrous, they put in. One did not need the image in order to commune with Lord and Savior. They fortified this attitude with the first three of the Ten Commandments.

Alonso was quiet. He took some time to let the pages of the album drift over his lap, the good wives and stacked offspring, his hands limp at his sides.

"And after a while, he looked us in the face and told us that there were only two commandments." Marisol named them. "Thou shalt not kill and Do no harm." She shrugged. "I said that sounded like a very broad definition of terms."

To which Alonso replied that this was the God who had brought him away. This was the God who had defined the terms, and that his God was the true

Maker and that all others were false. He went on to say that there could be no Redeemer because the very act of worship of another flesh and blood being was idolatrous in itself. He could not articulate much beyond that, and to Marisol, it had the cadence of rehearsal, of having heard it before many times and repeating it, as one would a rosary. She probed and gathered and tried to embrace her son and wept when he rose and shoved her.

"I fell off the couch," she said.

She collected herself.

She remembered having experienced sentiments nearly identical to those of Alonso's in recent years. While she revered the teachings of Jesus and reflected on them daily, Marisol had come to question what the difference was between the prophets of the Old Testament and the Savior, or the rabbis of Jewish Aggadah, or the saints of the One, Holy, Roman, Catholic and Apostolic Church in which she was raised. She read of Hanina ben Dosa and Honi the Circle Maker, who had lived and operated in Galilee during the same era. Neither of them made quite the splash that Christ had, she allowed ruefully, though they had accomplished more or less the same feats. Hanina ben Dosa's devotion healed the sick and made bread appear in an empty oven. Honi the Circle Maker prayed for rain and when he got it asked God to lessen or increase the rainfall by varying degrees.

"I'd like to conclude that there are no miracle

workers, only encounters," Marisol started, hesitated, and finished, "but I can't. I'd be opening myself up to the wackiness of alien abductions. Did you know that some folks actually said that's what happened to my son? That a UFO picked him up? Because there was no trace when he went." She scoffed.

Later that night, she found Alonso on his father's laptop, two windows open, one running *Myst*, the other his mother's Facebook page.

She stated that she never signed out as it was a sort-of joint account for herself and her husband. She asked what he was up to and he told her that he was looking for pictures of Aleah from church. He did not remember her last name. Marisol, pleased that Alonso had begun to take an interest in reconnecting with familiar faces, looked her up and found her under her Friends list. She asked if he would like help in setting up his own Facebook account. He declined.

"The next day I wanted to upload some photos that we'd taken with the digital camera. I went into the Photos app, section, area—I don't know—and I saw hundreds and hundreds of images, all of the same person."

Of Aleah?

"Of Aleah, yes."

Pulled from Facebook?

"I'm sure. I don't think they said but two words to each other since he came home. And before, when he was a little boy, he'd been a shepherd, I guess, to the younger ones. But I don't know if he'd ever favored her over anyone else. Why? What did he do?"

Allred McKnight told his parents that he was unable to see, hear, or smell. His father, a doctor, and his mother, a Ph.D. candidate, said that this was impossible, as he was looking at them and responding to them as a sighted and hearing person does. His stepfather asked him to follow the tiny dot of a penlight with his eyes, which he did, and there did not appear to be any cloudiness, indicating retinal detachment. As for his hearing, his mother vouched for her son's tendency to surround himself in their old CDs, tapes, and LPs, his headphones fixed and gently vibrating with basslines of Genesis, Grace Jones, Paul McCartney's "Band on the Run".

His parents began taking him on short outings around his old haunts. Often, though when grocery shopping had been done for the week, they would take him to the HEB three miles from their house and walk with him through the aisles. According to his mother, Allred could move through the store unassisted, if supervised. She was wont to point out things that might spark his interest, the sushi bar and its workers assembling spicy tuna rolls or a bright arrangement of balloons at the florist's. His headphones were usually locked in place and he obediently swallowed the free samples given him by the people at the sushi bar. He could direct the coin-operated claw machine, one of the few in years to receive from it a prize, a plush Pikachu.

As for his olfactory sense, this was harder to gauge, and it was what distressed him over and above his claims of blindness and deafness. When he could no longer smell, his mother said, his wariness of her husband and herself increased. He started as though electrocuted when she came up behind without warning. He snapped, out of habit, jaw cracking, teeth snapping, once, when his stepfather called his name and, yielding no response, approached him to tap him on the shoulder. His sojourns through the supermarket were made with one hand along the shelves, disregarding any items that crashed to the floor. His parents tailed him closely, one to pick up the spillage, the other to direct him away from sharp corners or stray shopping carts.

What made his alleged decline particularly baffling was his simultaneous improvement in other respects. For one, his posture was now nearly upright. For another, his feet and hands were now distinguishable from one another and his urge to climb the highest summit he could find when frightened had lessened. His voice was clearer and louder. He was reluctant to speak, but when he did, he communicated with articulation, if only to his parents and to his general practitioner, precise, unsure, like a foreigner negotiating a new language.

Paul the GP asked him about his inability to

smell. "Do you mean, you're not able to smell anything at all?"

Allred said, "No."

"No, you can't smell anything at all? Or, No, that's not what you meant?"

"No, that's not what I meant."

"Do you think your sense of smell isn't as strong as it used to be?"

"No."

"Can you tell me a little more about that?"

"I mean, it's different."

"Different in what way?"

Allred thought. He breathed awhile, and pronounced, "Different in a way that has altered everything else."

"Your eyes and your ears?"

"Yes. My eyes and ears are altered as a result."

"Can you tell me some more about that?"

"My sense of smell informs me of what my eyes and ears cannot."

"In what way does it inform you?"

"Whether people mean what they say they mean."

Paul reminded him of facial expressions and tone of voice, and that smell was not a sense that people often used to determine emotion or intent. Allred replied that this was untrue and that it had been a necessary trait in order to abide by the customs. Paul asked if he might elaborate on these customs.

"From what I could understand," the GP said, "that is, initially, he was describing what sounded to me like standard issue traits of autism—the inability to read faces or pick up on vocal tones. And of course, these are also symptoms of trauma. But signs of autism would have appeared much earlier than this, and his parents remember him, as I remember him, to be a friendly, outgoing kid. And this was not post-traumatic. It seemed that the trauma was here, now, among us. He sat closer to the door this time and was keeping an eye on the window. My office is on the third floor. I tried not to move too suddenly, and I sat in front of the window, should he get any ideas about jumping out. And anyway, they were locked. I mentioned these things to him, if he had heard of autism or PTSD, and when I tried to describe them more fully, he shook his head and told me that wasn't it either."

What Allred had said was that his sense of smell without its former keenness was useless to him now, as were his ears and eyes. He said that without it, it was impossible to know precisely what anyone was feeling, therefore thinking, at any given time. He said that before, there had only been six people. Now, there were many.

"Before," Paul began. "Before you came home?"

"Yes."

"Where did you live before you came home? The last time we got together, you told me that you lived outside."

"I'm not sure. In the woods."

"In the woods around here? Close by?"

"I don't know."

"You lived with six other people?"

"No, five others. I was the sixth."

"Did you live in a house? Or some kind of dwelling?"

"No."

"So, you did, in fact, live completely outside?"

"Yes. Among the elements."

"Why did you live outside?"

"We were commanded to."

"Commanded by whom? It wasn't a choice?"

"No. We were there of our own volition. But we were commanded to live in the woods."

"Commanded by whom?"

"The God."

"The god of the woods?"

"No. The one God."

"I'm not sure what you mean."

"The God. The one you and I both know."

Paul the GP asked, "God spoke to you?"

Allred McKnight told him, "Yes. On two occasions."

"When?"

"Many years ago."

"God is not speaking to you now, the way we're speaking?"

"He would never be so crude."

"God is a he?" The GP recounted being taken aback by the remark, however undeterred from posing more questions.

Allred allowed that this aspect of the entity was difficult to determine, as it manifested differently each time. Paul wanted to know how he was able to identify a being that was a constant shape-shifter; he asked how this being showed itself.

"Sometimes he is a he. Sometimes she is a she. Sometimes he is a tree. Sometimes he is a bee."

The rhyming cadence interested Paul. Was the subject trying to be funny? Or was it involuntary? To which Allred, whether he knew it or not, quoted Exodus or Popeye: "I am what I am."

"You, too, are God?"

"Sometimes he is me."

"Would he show himself physically? The way I'm sitting in front of you now and you're sitting in front of me?"

"Once."

"Just once."

"Yes. The rest were in dreams."

"Was it the same for the other five people you lived with?"

"Yes."

"Allred, I'm going to ask you a few more questions."

"All right."

"Do you—or did you when you lived in the woods and even before that, before you left—did you sometimes hear voices? By that, I mean, did you hear voices while there was no one else in the room with you?"

"Impossible. The God was there."

"But you did not always see him."

"No."

"Except when you were dreaming."

"Yes."

"Did the others you live with see or hear this being more often than you?"

"It was not the custom to boast of that."

"Boast of what."

"One does not boast of favor from the God. One ought to not be so crude. Frequency of contact is no indication of favor. One hears and one listens. That is all."

"I'm not accusing anyone of boasting. I'm just trying to put this together."

"One ought not to do that either."

"To do what?"

"Put it together."

"Is God here with us now?"

"I don't know."

"Because you can't see, hear, or smell?"

"Yes."

"Allred, do you believe you have special abilities?"

"How so?"

"Can you do things that other people would consider impossible?"

"Nothing is impossible. To say otherwise is crude."

"I'll put it differently: Can you do things that other people might not be able to do? Like predict the future or walk on water?"

"No." Allred swallowed. There had been a brief interval between questionings in which Paul went into the hall to buy snacks from the vending machine, and the subject ate from the small bag of barbecue chips one morsel at a time, steady, barely chewing. He was halfway through the bag when he amended the statement to include his sightings of others in his number who had.

Paul asked, putting his own chips aside, salt and vinegar. "You saw people walk on water?"

"No. Other things."

"Predict the future?"

"Yes."

"Can you give me an example?"

"No."

"Do you mean, No you don't remember?"

"No."

"No, you're not allowed?"

"Yes."

"Can you tell me why you're not allowed?"

"It would interfere. It is not the God's business to

interfere."

Here, in a moment wherein professional conduct blurred and fascination came into sharp relief, Paul told him that by commanding Allred to leave his family and live in the woods was an act of interference in itself. He imagined that God would know the agony of a missing child, as any parent would.

To which, Allred intoned, "The God's ways are not our ways. It is crude to impose other notions."

Paul asked if Allred thought that anyone was out to get him.

"I don't know."

"Because you can no longer see, hear, or smell, correct?"

"I don't know what you want from me."

"I'm not here to hurt you."

"I don't know that."

"And your mom and Joel aren't going to hurt you."

"I don't know that either."

"What makes you think that?"

They had come together by increments over the course of their discussion, moving at first toward one another in the middle of the GP's office. Now, the subject had retreated to his original position at the start of the appointment, by the door. Paul made sure to position himself as a block to the window, if things came to that.

He had known Joel McKnight as an

underclassman in college. They had gone to medical school together. He stood up as Joel's best man, wishing a bright future upon his new bride and their son. Their son, who had played with his children who had minced and turned and pirouetted alongside him in "Dancin' Man", who sat before the GP now as though he had never set foot upon this wicked planet in all its secularity before.

He asked Allred what was wicked or who.

Allred told him that everything was wicked. It was full of noise. It was full of smells. Everyone seemed to know things about him that he did not, things which he had not authorized, and that it was cruel that the information was so one-sided, that though they knew him, he did not know them.

Paul reminded him that his parents had only told a select few, perhaps but no more than ten people, that he had returned. It was impossible for everyone to know everything about him.

Allred's parents had raised him with God.

Paul asked later, more to the corner of the ceiling emblazoned with the pink and green light reflected from the decorative prism in the window, "What do you do if it isn't a God you recognize? It might be heresy to define the issue any which way. I might be doing the patient a disservice by allowing the delusion to continue. If it is one."

He reminded Allred before the two parted that the younger man had spoken of there being too many sounds and too many smells.

"Too many lights, too," Allred added.

Paul asked him how these things could be if Allred could not see, hear, or smell.

While Allred did not have an answer, Paul supplied a story from the Talmud concerning four rabbis that had ascended to heaven, body and soul. One went mad. One denounced God. One died. One and only one survived to tell the tale.

In retrospect, Paul said, "I shouldn't have told him that story. His parents said I was wrong to have told him that story. It was unprofessional. It fed the illness."

Allred reminded him that while three of their number had died, two emerged from the woods with him.

Julian, according to her mother, had never been much of a dog person. In fact, despite a personality that otherwise consisted of a lot of bravado and vinegar, Julian Livingstone was afraid of dogs. As a child, she feigned disinterest when the neighborhood children brought their pit bull with them on playdates and hid in the house, under the guise of finding more amusing activities than humoring what she called a "dumb old dog". She visibly cowered at the sight of her late grandmother's teacup terrier, Missy, a creature that, because of her small size, perceived threats everywhere and snarled accordingly.

And yet, in her days home after her absence, Julian kept company with the family's boxer mix. The dog answered to Jules, and was acquired about fifteen years after their eldest daughter's disappearance. They insisted the shelter had named the dog. Jules answered to Julian, unused to a similar name, as Julian answered to her parents' beckoning of the dog in much the same fashion, head erect, ears perked. They slept together in the dog's crate, which was large enough to accommodate both if they overlapped, say, with one's head resting atop the other's reclining form.

"To train her to do anything before would've been impossible," her mother said.

Julian Livingstone before her disappearance had been difficult. Here was a child that would only follow orders if the mood suited her. Here was an impious creature that refused to wear shoes, to the store, to school, to church, as though the apparatuses were designed for the sole purpose of her discomfort and inconvenience. Behold a child that had been brought up in what could unanimously be considered a good home, and observe as she complies with your request to put her shoes on in the car and honors it so far as to make it through the parking lot, only to kick them off once her feet have touched the linoleum inside the supermarket. Watch her as she watches you swell with tangible rage, as she knows that you know how foul you must look to passersby, a bad parent. You invent a taunting interior monologue for her, in which she poses questions along the lines of "What are you going to do? Hit me?"

Was Julian Livingstone capable of violence?

Her mother sighed. "No. Previously, no. Her sisters adored her. They adored her over us. We liked to joke—I suppose semi-joke—that they were in cahoots. She always got them whispering together, and shut them up as soon as one of us stepped into the room. We told them they were never going to get away with whatever they were going to get away with because they always looked like they were up to something."

Was the mother afraid of the daughter?

The mother allowed that it was much in the same way that you fear an animal you've brought in from the wild. She added, too, that Julian had been her "late-in-life" child, and viewed the birth, without self-consciousness, independently of any union between herself and her husband, of any intention. Julian had heralded the coming of Susanna and Teresa shortly thereafter, no one else. Their mother was forty-eight years old and relegated to a fate she thought she had escaped with age. She stopped usage of the pill at around thirty-five, as recommended by her physician, and a decade of the rhythm method resulting in a monthly period that could be counted on as regularly as a Swiss watch reassured the notion that she and her husband would live a life uninterrupted. Her arrogance, which had swelled in this time, as wide around and as pink as a bubble gum balloon, burst at a routine checkup, the doctor the archangel carrying a urine sample, affirming the Anunciation.

"I worked in data analysis," she said of her life before.

Imagine the opposite of routine, she said of the impious creature who refused to put on her shoes at the HEB.

The legend: Rather than comply with her mother's insistence and damnations, Julian had taken first one shoe and then the other and, upon entering the produce aisle, hurled one shoe and then the other at a large pyramid of pomegranates. The aisle was small and the pomegranates were many, sneaky, rolling underfoot and under carts, upsetting the gait of shoppers on walkers, projectile, felling glass vases on display at the florist's, scattering petals, shedding blood from those who caught themselves in the act of picking everything up.

To all of this, the impious creature shrugged and told her mother, as well as the infant Teresa in the baby seat of the shopping cart, that she stood on holy ground. It would be unfitting to wear shoes on holy ground.

Julian Livingstone had been enamored with that portion of Exodus, wherein Moses is commanded by a burning bush to remove his sandals in its presence.

Her mother remained sour. She sniffed, "Well. I

was unaware that the HEB on Sydney Baker Street in Kerrville was sacred. The outlet on Main was the first of the franchise, you'd think that would be the place." Her voice was thick with irony. "Maybe if anyone had told me, I'd have shown more reverence."

The legend: Following the destruction of the pomegranate pyramid, the mother abandoned the impious creature.

"Abandoned," the mother scoffed. "I let her stew while Terri and I got the shopping done. I told Jules to come with me, she wouldn't budge, I told her, See you later, and went first to apologize to the nearest manager I could find. I don't mind telling you that I was more than capable of finagling our way out of having to pay for all that bruised fruit. After that, I figured I'd see Jules again once we'd made our rounds and we'd reconcile at checkout. I had little tantrums, too. It was what my mother did. It gave us both time to cool off."

The hour of that shopping trip was late, the store about to close. All the while, the mother had kept an eye out and caught sight of the creature several times between the pyramid crash and checkout, if in glimpses. She knew that Julian was on the move, having spotted her in the cereal aisle, in pet food, once covertly peeling back the foil on a container of yogurt to taste. The creature opened boxes and scattered crumbs. She could easily be found. It was no surprise to her mother when the creature did not appear at the cash registers. The mother had the store page her; she soon recognized its futility, for Julian was as a cat, answering to her name if the whim moved her. She had the checkers walk the trail of crumbs. All that remained of the creature were her shoes, still at opposite ends of the produce aisle.

Her mother declared it a rapture, again terribly facetious. A rapture was her husband's word, in reference to their daughter's vanishing from her bedroom a short time later. His wife now lifted her hands in mock worship of this gospel. For a while, he was of the opinion that the supermarket flight was something that they ought to take as a prelude of what was to come.

But, as her mother stated twenty years later, "She was in the wall. I mean, she'd found her way into the back, the storage area, and figured out a way to get into the crawl space. And get herself out. As soon as the nighttime manager had axed his way in, she was gone again. When I say axed, I mean with an axe, that the store is supposed to use in case of a fire, or something. Somehow, amidst all this excitement, she'd communicated to the manager that she didn't want to leave, that she did not want to go home, that she would stay right where she was and live on cereal and bruised pomegranates. The staff looked at me as though I was some kind of monster."

The child had said no such thing, with regards to cereal or anything else. This was fiction. This was to placate. In fact, once the child had vanished into the wall, there was not hide nor hair of her. It might have been easy for her mother to dismiss this as unruly behavior from a disobedient creature, as well as the notion that if a soul does not want to be found, she will, by any means necessary, stay hidden. The manager had actually lost track of the creature for a good twenty-five minutes, which he, in turn, had not communicated to her irate mother. For those twenty-five minutes, he heard not one sound. At first, he assumed the worst, that the child had taken a wrong turn, mis-stepped onto a fragile portion of the floor and plummeted into the basement, crippled, unconscious, perhaps dead. He crept along with his ear to the wall so that he might detect a scratching from the other side or a shout from below. He told the staff to keep the mother where she was. He ordered them not to call any emergency numbers, for he was as afraid of a lawsuit as Mrs. Livingstone was of judgement by righteous young people in red polo shirts.

It was when the night manager had given up calling and knocking and raised the axe, tearing up the wall in an effort to wedge himself in to drag the child out himself, that the creature reappeared. She stood not one foot away; her crown grazed the axe's raised, blunt end. She did not speak; she sniffed, the way one does to draw attention and when she had it, she asked the manager what day it was. She wanted to know if it was still Friday. She wanted to know how many days it had been. Nothing about her was changed, save for a tousled, windblown look to her hair and a fine layer of grit over her face. There was a smear of sticky red around her mouth, which the manager determined to be fruit juice, possibly pomegranate. Her feet were blistered on the bottom, some had burst, some healing over with new, papery scales. She smelled strange—but then, most children did. He chalked it up to tomboy exploration, the thrill of illicit creeping and spying. He asked if she was hurt, besides her feet. She shook her head, then asked how her sister was. The manager reminded her that she had only been gone for less than half-an-hour, that her mother and Teresa were just outside, waiting for her. She nodded, ruminating, running her tongue over the sticky red, as if to confirm to no one but herself that it was still there.

Her mother performed fiery outrage at her eldest daughter's mischief. Mrs. Livingstone wanted the staff of the HEB on Sydney Baker Street to know and feel her wrath, for someone had to have a direct experience, aside from herself. She bided her time, in wait for an incident that would cement her proof, to God, to her husband, to one and all that this impious creature should never have been born to her. It took almost nine years, but she was consummately sure, at the time, that she had it.

And in fact, what did she have? An act of

rebellion, yes. But what child has not misbehaved in a supermarket? Children have had tantrums resulting in expensive property damage, for much less, for Oreos. How often has a child gone missing, moments after you deserted them in the produce aisle with a chilly dismissal of "See you later"?

"She pretended not to recognize me when they brought her out from the back," Mrs. Livingstone put in, twenty years into the future, though the past remained in keen circulation. "The manager asked her, pointing to me, Is this your mommy? That child never called me Mommy in her life. She called me Margaret over and above any other moniker." Mrs. Livingstone paused to calm herself. "And Jules looked at me, blinking. And she said, I guess so. She actually—this gets me still—she asked the manager if this was the same lady she'd come into the store with."

Had Julian Livingstone recognized her sister?

Mrs. Livingstone recounted that while it had taken a minute, her eldest seemed to shake some of whatever held her in its grip and grew clear-eyed when Teresa, not quite three, pronounced what she could of her name. A syllable, inaccurate: Choo. Recalling to mind a choo-choo train, indicative of Jules.

"That's when she decided she would come home with us," their mother said.

When reminded of how she ran to her impious child twenty years later, her exclamation and exaltation uttered in the same breath to form her daughter's name: JULES—Margaret Livingstone said that it would've felt blasphemous otherwise.

"If I'd stayed in bed," she mused, "if I'd told her to leave, to go back to wherever she'd come from. Well. David wouldn't have stood for it. You don't treat your own kid like a ghost." Here, she reared back in imitation of Old Testament, rabbinical foresight. "Now. Look you what's happened."

The Enamorados, following a Sunday service to find their son missing the moment they had their backs turned in the parking lot, feared again his disappearance. This would have evoked an agony sharper than before, for it had been so soon that they had Alonso back that he was lost again. They searched the environs, a neighborhood that boasted two parks, one with a spacious, shaded playground, the other a dam that tamed the overflow from the Guadalupe River and which Sunday strollers often found themselves walking across on a hot day.

It was where Marisol found her son, in the act of disrobing. Though he had an audience of parkgoers, he was down to his socks when his mother called for him, and the act was nonchalant, almost oblivious. When Marisol rushed to block his nakedness from dumbfounded eyes and leering children, he, of all people, seemed to find her behavior uncouth, the dumbfounded eyes and leering children coarse. An argument ensued, wherein she urged her son to dress at once. Her son hissed. She ordered him to speak, the language of English or Spanish was his choice. Again, he hissed, then spat. The exchange culminated in Alonso pushing, rushing, once again on all fours, faster than he had ever maneuvered on two legs, into the river and through the fanned water that cascaded over the dam. Here, he immersed himself three times before standing upright, his organs on full and extended display. He reared back, his arms spread, as though this were his stage, in anticipation of the parkgoers' wild applause. Where he might have heard their halloos and hurrahs privately (or, at the very least, imagined them), his assemblage was silent, save for one or two giggling youngsters. One of whom was keen to point out his erection, for which her mother or wrangler admonished her, murmuring something to the effect of the man being unwell, clarifying when the child pressed further, that the man was sick in his mind.

"I could've died right there," Marisol affirmed.

Her husband, unable now to negotiate the park's uneven, hilly terrain, sat in the car with the air conditioner on and a window cracked for good measure, missing the whole incident. The radio played Wings' song that changed three times, "Band on the Run".

Marisol noted that it was the first time she had seen her son freed of the doom-and-gloom suspicion, the vigilance, since he had been home. It was almost a relief that he had not posed that dreaded question: "Are you going to kill me?" He had asked at home and at church, in public and before she put out the light in his bedroom. Once, he had asked well within earshot of the drive-thru operator at the Burger King, just as they were sorting through Whoppers and fries. The drive-thru operator took it for criticism about the food and made a jolly remark that Alonso must be a health nut. Marisol drove away, abandoning her debit card.

On this day, with an open-mouthed, goggle-eyed congregation in his captivity, he bore himself to all dangers, real and fantastic, eschewing *that* question for a head-on approach. Were he to speak, his words would have been in cackling defiance. He danced in the water, which rippled around his groin, and dared his mother to face him, here and now.

"Are you going to kill me?" became "Come and take it".

Marisol, a daily Bible scholar, could not help but make the comparison between her son and the ecstasy of King David, who also stripped and danced as he paraded the Ark of the Covenant through the streets of Jerusalem. On this day, she was astonished—less so for her son's recklessness than toward the masses, the picnic-goers and weekenders who seemed fixed in place, lifting not one finger to call someone (Call who? An ambulance? The police? To report what? A 5150, the way they did on television?). They looked to her suddenly uncharitable mind like a lot of smug-faced morons. When a child laughed, a small boy no more than nine, she did not hesitate to turn him to her by the root of the hair on his crown, all the easier for her to slap him, once, twice, three times before delivering a heavier blow that would send him to the ground and summon his mother. Just as easily, Marisol pushed the woman away and warned her by showing her wheel of keys, one for the car, one for the house, one for the church, fanned in her fingers like blades. She would put the woman's eyes out with them, should she get close enough.

When the weekenders and picnic-goers had taken a few steps back, Marisol removed her shoes and waded into the river, Sunday best be damned, to retrieve her son. From the bank, she detected a hum that was barely lucid, hysterical, someone shrieking. She turned to find that it was the mother she had shown her keys to, hovering now over her wailing boy, both mimicking outrage, disingenuous, clinging to one another, swiping at crocodile tears, bitches the two of them, the woman's voice a staticky jumble until a phrase would make itself clear in her performance, something like, "How DARE you?"

"It made me laugh," Marisol said.

And hers was a witch's laugh, issuing louder than she thought it could through her small form, only five-foot-one. She felt it in her chest. It would not stop. It was deeper than her usual sound of mirth, which had always been closer to a polite titter, akin to Minnie Mouse. This, she understood, was the real thing. And it continued, mocking, as she went further, up to her waist.

There was no Ark.

What was so funny?

Marisol said, "I remember very clearly reading in a Judy Blume book when I was young—I forget which one—but someone in it says that it's very silly to laugh if you don't know what the joke is. I think it was a bullying teacher or something."

She thought Alonso had seen only her as she called and drew herself deeper into the water. The Guadalupe's bottom was deceptive, with rocks that were either too slick to gain purchase on or too sharp, both a deterrent for barefoot adventurers. There was a rumor of a snapping turtle, of territorial fish that bit. To Marisol, this was several steps beyond civilization as she knew it, and the resentment of having to cross this demarcation, from order to yelping unreason, inspired what she referred to as "ugly thoughts" toward her son. She raised her hand, and she did her best to soften her jaw, to extend all appendages in gestures of goodwill and step into the costume of gentle motherhood, as an actor would, so that Alonso might be swayed, all the easier for his mother to snatch him and haul him to the riverbank before any further humiliation ensued.

Marisol gritted now her teeth. "And, by golly, I thought I had him. But who do you think happened to be there that day? Who else?"

Alonso, looking beyond his mother's hand, dazed and obedient. For there, ankle deep, her hem submerged and her skirt ballooning over the running water, was Aleah. Aleah, which came from the Hebrew, *Aliyah,* to mean "ascent", with pertinence to the Jews making their return from widespread scattering to find themselves home at last. Aleah, twenty-four or twenty-five, at one's peak, wherein experience and capability and beauty merge, which can be achieved only once in a lifetime and never again, who stood with her shoes on the riverbank pointed to this exchange, herself in a dress of bronze satin from the Gap, having only to call Alonso's name to make him come to her.

He did, calmed if not chastened.

Had this performance been for her?

That inner mechanism, which in Marisol wound to project all the actions and verses of a righteous woman, locked and would not budge. The saintly automaton had broken. In its place was a live creature that coughed on urine-sour water and choked, "Fuck it." She let Aleah take the helm. On dry land, she snatched up her shoes and her purse, barked once at the bitch mother and her bitchier son when she met their eye, and stalked up the hill to the parking lot.

Trudging, fuming, Marisol heard herself passing

curses upon Aleah. She marveled at how clearly now the girl stood in her mind's eye, whereas before, the girl's presence had been a vague one, at best. Marisol taught her in Sunday school; there was a watery vision, a lesson on Passover and Easter, teaching the children the significance of the salted water, the bitter herbs, the boiled egg, the lamb bone, the saltine crackers for the matzoh that HEB didn't carry, Aleah at eight or nine working the DVD player to show the class *The Prince of Egypt*, Val Kilmer as Moses and Ralph Fiennes as the Pharoah. Marisol wished plagues upon her.

Why?

Marisol was quick to answer. "He went to her, not me. I was practically submerged. I'm not a strong swimmer, I never have been, and he knew that. She didn't even want to get her dress wet."

Then, hearing herself, she paused. "I don't suppose it helped at all that when I got back to the car, I found his father had up and left, too."

The car radio played Earth, Wind, and Fire's devotional hit, and Marisol's husband had wandered away into the trees, as if in answer to one or many people calling his name. It was during these moments that he would, in fact, forget his name and much of the world as he knew it. Its conventions baffled him. He was confounded at the volume of people he did not know who seemed to know him, too intimately for his liking. One might have said that his brain was wrapped around and around in a lot of sticky gauze, which would evaporate and materialize again for unknown, though he understood, good reason. He was pleased when the gauze came and he could shirk the years. He might have called it a liberation. He was again a child, let to walk farther and hide more now that he operated from within the costume of a grown man six feet tall. He did not look ill. He sought the familiar. His wants were specific.

And he did not go far. Though lucid moments were, these days, fewer, he remained ambulatory, enough to brave one hill without trouble. Here was a portion of the park that was bought by the city in more recent years. Before, he knew, it had been something else. He could often jog his memory by recognizing what a thing was not, or had not been. For one, it had not been a neighborhood, though there had been houses. For another, there had been people. Marisol had been there, though there were no children, not yet.

Today, if you went down the hill's western slope and into the trees, you could largely ignore the noise from town. If you followed the path and did not look back, with knee-high grass on either side and sunflowers in the warmer months and possumhaw holly in winter, you could very easily imagine the world as you knew it to have dropped away. Of course, there were clues of a prior civilization, these guideposts with colored markings to indicate which way to the birdhouses, which way to the pond, watermarked or sun baked or molested by wild things. Where the path ended, you found yourself at a gate, chain-link, that was twice your height. The rust on the lattices had spread, long ago, to the bar that kept it locked and in place. It would not do to try it. You were the first human to have laid eyes on this place in ages.

Beyond the gate, Alonso's father peered through the overgrowth, and caught sight of a flight of stairs that wound around the greenery and up another hill. They were made from a mix of concrete and caliche. You could see, if you had the eyes for it, fragments of shells embedded in each step, leftover from the days when the park and its environs were part and parcel of an ancient ocean.

He started when he saw a pair of legs descending, first the Land's End all-weather slip-on shoes, then the blue jeans, much like what he wore now. He had it briefly in his head that he was watching himself come down from the top of that hill at some future time, and that he was observing from a period long before cars and radios, but after the flood. He did not fear the liopleurodon, nor the saber-toothed tiger. He wanted to know what this creature in the all-weather shoes was capable of. He was still, and when the rest of the biped revealed himself (for it was also a man), he stared.

The other man stopped and, knowing that there

were eyes on him, followed an odor or an inkling until he found his company.

There ensued, in the time it took to take a breath, the feeling that one or the other of them might pounce, to claim territory, at the very least, to assert himself. They forgot manners and conventions, and there was no one else to remind them.

But it passed. It passed when Alonso's father recalled the first lines of a song, and recalled that song having played on a radio, and the radio having been in his car. He called out, pitch-perfect, "Dr. Livingstone, I presume" and abandoned the rest when it did not come. He knew that it was the Moody Blues, following the logic that if he knew it, the other man would know it, too.

The man, instead, scowled. "That's me, yes."

Alonso's father shook his head.

The man approached the gate, his fingers looping through the links. "David Livingstone, that's me. Can I help you?"

"Julian told me this," her father said. He spoke with gravity, as though it were dispensed from on high. Describing these particular events, he did not want to believe otherwise, or he could not.

"Where she had lived before, she just called the woods. But she would tell me about it, little by little, if there was no one else around. I hesitate to call myself privileged. But she told me, first of all, that she emerged from that place through the park. There is only one park, the one we went to all the time, for swimming and hikes. We would get Burger King or Jimmy John's and make a picnic there by the dam. I knew it was the same place because she described the gate and the steps coming down. I asked if she went up or down those steps to get home. She said down."

David Livingstone, on the precept of going into town to run errands for the family cookout, forsook those invented duties and drove to the park. He pulled into the entrance where the memorial bench was installed. The hydrangeas were drying up, the blooms papery and brown. He brushed up against one, barely grazing it, scattering petals. "I don't know why we put those in," he said of them. "They come from France or someplace, they're too delicate for way out here." He took the path that looped around into the shade where the playground and the tennis courts were. It was too hot for sport but not for play, and a few families lounged at the picnic tables while their children thumped around the wooden turrets and hanging bridges. He went around three times before continuing toward the wider, common route which led to the pool and the public grills and a grassy expanse where his neighbors from Bangladesh liked to play cricket, turning off at the sign directing the way to the birdhouses and the wildflower exhibit and the pond, passing a plaque put in by the city in memoriam of the park's major donors, another plaque marking an archeological or historical event unknown to David Livingstone because he'd never stopped to read it, the dam where a small crowd had gathered at the river's edge, the river itself, the smaller playground which had a sandbox and a troop of animal swings in close formation, more public grills, the park office and restrooms, ending up at the point of outset, the bench.

At home, Julian remained in diapers, though she was close to thirty. She slept in the same bed as the dog, who was also called Jules. She refused to speak more than what she could mimic, save for what little she told him about the woods.

In the woods, there was lush green in every direction. There was warmth enough to forgo clothes. There was only one season, one of fecundity. In the woods, you ate from the trees and from what the ground yielded. Fruit abounded. The colors were bright. You minded your neighbors and they minded you. To get to it, you began at the top of the stairs and went down.

Do no harm.

Thou shalt not kill.

Those were the laws for living in the woods.

"And that's all she would tell me about it," David Livingstone said. But, as he amended, "There were a lot of rules."

These were many, often repetitive. When fruit could be picked. When it could not be picked. When one slept. When one could not sleep. Where one could sleep. Where one could not sleep. His daughter grew impatient with her father's prying and went silent on that or any other subject. He'd had to condense them, and in this way, he could extract the values.

In the woods, there was no speech, for it prevented lying.

There was no hoarding, for it prevented jealousy and upset, avoiding a situation wherein one has more than the others.

There was no intimacy, for it prevented violence and jealousy. See hoarding.

There were no clothes, for humans did not sin until they put on clothes. See hoarding and intimacy.

Was this how the squirrels in the park lived, as well as beasts in the true wilderness? Was the idea of animal instinct a lot of romantic folly, and the bats and the bees and the deer operated according to a deliberate, unshakable code, whereby you watched and were also being watched? Or else? Face a trial by a jury of your peers? Face the wild alone? Were you expelled or were you devoured? To whom did you appeal? To whom did you report?

At first, David Livingstone did not see the stairs when he reached the top of the hill. He went to the place he judged the summit to be and turned there in all directions before catching sight of the river. This branch had dried out and curved along the gate like a trench, and it was flanked on both sides by very old, very dry cypresses. He went down this way, his steps slow, deliberate, and as opposed to walking the bank, he clambered down into the trench itself and plodded on through the middle. His shoes kicked up dust. There were shreds of hardened grass, the muddied, silver bones of minnow-fish.

Too, there was a keen feeling of having an audience. If not eyes, there were other faculties that knew his presence and held back. Of course, it was a sanctuary, the birdhouse fields were near. Squirrels would follow a hiker if you had snacks to share, and a whole pack of them would trail you to your car if you were too generous, and the begging could turn monstrous on a dime. Possums nested here and, contrary to their sweetness, would finish anything off with a claw or a fang if it drew too close. Bobcats wandered in from the true wilderness to hunt the them and the squirrels that fattened on granola and mixed nuts. Snakes kept the lesser rodents at bay and the bats consumed their fill of bugs when the sun went down. They lived to eat. They went quiet before they pounced.

David Livingstone said, "I can't say that I feared losing my life to a possum that day. Or anything else. Only that I was being watched."

Were the woods quiet?

"Very. Save for me and my noise."

Had David Livingstone been afraid?

"I think they were more frightened of me, as is

the usual way. But I suppose if a number of critters got together, they could have carried me off and eaten me alive. They aren't bound by the same laws as us. I don't think anything would stop them. Thankfully, they're not so organized."

It made him think, not so much of his daughter's rules for living in the woods. Rather, the walk uphill and down, and now, around and around the trench within open detection of so many hidden creatures that peered from the cypresses and the grass and dark caches in the dirt, he considered those rules which were self-imposed. These were not dictated by scripture. They were not in accordance with the laws of the United States or of any other nation. These were what kept David Livingstone contained, for David Livingstone and handed down by David Livingstone alone. If you wanted to call civilization the woods, he imagined that they would easily apply here as there. If you wanted to call either place civilized, which he was sometimes reluctant to do with the former.

These were:

Never yearn so much for company that you would do anything to keep it.

Never let anyone know your honest opinion.

Never whisper or write down what you would do in a compromising situation.

Never make friends, but present yourself as a necessary and affable addition to any group.

Never say that you are one thing.

Never say how much money you have.

Never instigate gossip, but gather it, should you need it at a later time.

Never shit where you eat.

Never apologize unless the lack of an apology will be the worse for you.

"This must all sound very reptilian," David Livingstone mused. "But if your experience was mine, you would agree. It works."

The trench was six feet deep and accommodated crowds of inner tubers in the days following a downpour when it could still be hot enough to immerse yourself completely. The heat now, one hundred degrees on a good day, discouraged David Livingstone from going around more than he thought necessary. It might have been five or six times. He thought he saw that zig-zag outline, indicative of stairs, on the hill's eastern end, and clambered out. He returned to the summit gritty all over. It was when he'd been ready to give up that he saw the top step. Having shaken his head and pounded dust and grass from his person and, not focusing on anything, landed on it with his bleary eye, he waded again through the brush, off the path, coming to the first in a winding flight down the hill.

He noted key moments.

"About halfway down, I heard water running. I didn't look, but I knew if I did, that the river would be as full as it had ever been. I didn't look because I didn't believe it.

"About that time, I did look up. I had to because I needed to see where I was going. I looked up and everything that had been dry was green. I smelled fruit. I looked up and I saw fruit hanging low and heavy from one of the trees. I don't know if it was a pear or a peach or a persimmon. I didn't touch it. I didn't touch it because I was afraid that it would go away if I did touch it.

"The rest of the world had fallen away. I was no longer in a park. Texas was not yet a state, or it had long ceased to be one. I considered going back up to the top of the hill to see if there were still houses. I'm not sure what I would've preferred, if the houses had been there or if they had vanished."

When had David Livingstone gone blind?

And for how long had it lasted?

"It was about the time I heard someone say, Dr. Livingstone, I presume."

He, like Alonso's father, recognized it foremost as a hit by the Moody Blues. He knew it secondly by the famed accounts of the nineteenth century Protestant missionary to Africa, who was greeted thus by a colleague, having seen no other white men around.

David Livingstone, in turn, was unable to describe the one who had addressed him. His vision had gone so suddenly that he could recall little more of his addressor than his dark hair and an estimation of being the same height as he.

"I said something to him," David Livingstone noted. "I don't remember what. I wonder if I'd said nothing to him. Or more so, if he'd said nothing to me. If he'd just let me be, it wouldn't have happened. I could say that I took what I had—have still—for granted, that I better appreciate what I have while I have it. I could say that I learned something about fellowship and trust, because he was the one who got me out of the park that day."

What were David Livingstone's first sensations, following his blindness?

He described an urge to descend on all fours, like a lesser creature, to the ground. The stairs were uneven and the terrain unpredictable; it would not do to have an additional injury, a broken bone, a concussion, another faculty lost. And, after a minute of groping the air, accompanied by growls and the foulest curses aimed at God, himself, and Alonso's father, he did descend and, like this, he made it in a crab-walk, down the stairs and to the gate. He went upright again and felt along the chain link until he found the bar which kept the gate shut. But panic made his palms and fingers sweaty, and he could get little purchase with them on an already rusted lock.

"I had a back-and-forth with him," he said of Alonso's father, not deigning to remember his name.

Alonso's father, no doubt puzzled by the predicament, was frozen in place, incapable of playing much more than a mild observer to a man who had looked at him with suspicion, as though he were the dangerous one, and then collapsing in a fit of swears and gnashing of teeth. No doubt puzzled, no doubt feeling that he was in the presence of a lunatic, he took a few cautious steps away from the gate. It seemed that David Livingstone blamed him for whatever had passed. It seemed that David Livingstone would harm him if he drew too close.

David Livingstone said, "I think it was when I cried and when I—when I—when my bladder let loose that he came back."

He was reluctant to credit Alonso's father much more than was due. He wondered aloud, without thinking, if Alonso's father was feeble-minded. He spoke disparagingly of the other man for some time before having to be reminded that it was, in fact, the other man, who managed to open the gate, which swung as though it had been oiled by his very touch, and who put David Livingstone's savage paw to his shoulder to guide him on the path.

David Livingstone maintained an aversion to helplessness. He claimed a repulsion for it. All incapacities, all disabilities were a result of one's own defective character, the very foundation of one's being, long before real development in the womb began. Accidents and illnesses were karmic, a word he would not have used, though the sentiment was the same. He attributed his successes, great and small, to his stubbornness or, using his word, bull-headedness. Such was his bullheadedness that if he felt there were too many ads for a product, whether they were on television or plugged as a YouTube sponsor, whether it was for antidepressants or luxury perfume, he would refuse to purchase it.

Had his bullheadedness been helpful to him?

"Yes," he said.

Even when Mr. Enamorado had to lead him from the changed woods to his car in the parking lot?

"Yes," David Livingstone said.

Even when Mr. Enamorado, thinking that he was driving David Livingstone home, in fact dropped him at the wrong house?

He was resolute, looking everywhere but where he ought. "Yes," even then.

For the car ride and before, though the parking lot and through the woods, David Livingstone was blind, though he yet could hear. What had he heard?

What had he heard in the woods?

He faltered. "The grass underfoot, crunching. Twigs snapping, I suppose. The river, I'm not sure. My guide was a fast walker and so we moved away from that area of the park very quickly. Birds. Squirrels."

What had he heard in the parking lot?

He guessed. "People. When I'd made my rounds, there was a crowd over by the dam, some commotion."

What had he heard in the car, while Mr.

Enamorado was on the road?

He remembered. "The radio. The classic rock station is what I have my own radio tuned to all the time, when it's just me. That Earth, Wind, and Fire song, the one that, I think, is just called 'Devotion'. Paul McCartney and Wings. That song—I forget who does it—that song that goes, *I been through the desert on a horse with no name.*" David Livingstone coughed. "And I felt the car stop. It didn't feel unusual, since I don't live far from the park. The distance felt right. I let myself out. I trusted he knew who I was."

Mr. Enamorado, of late, was diagnosed with early onset dementia. Was David Livingstone aware of that?

"No, I was not. I'd never seen him in my life before that day. I don't believe I have since."

About what time did David Livingstone regain his sight? Was it when he let himself out of the Enamorado's car? When he stepped onto the curb? Or when he walked up the front walkway and very nearly into the wrong house?

He was stiff, in body and in speech. He had no other advocate. "I stepped onto the curb. I heard the car pull away. No, I did not thank him, because he drove off before I could. I ask you to remember and understand what a jarring thing it is to be able to do something your whole lifetime and then have it taken away. I ask you to understand what it is to have stepped into a land of milk and honey one minute and pandemonium the next."

Describe the pandemonium.

"I was already up the walk and on the front steps. The houses in these neighborhoods look very alike. They're almost identical. I suppose one thing that might've tipped me off was that we have a rosemary bush in front of our house and this house didn't. I should've smelled the herb in the air. My mistake. I had my hand on the door, I was about to turn the knob and go in, when I felt—and saw—that the knob was already turning in my hand. I think that was when I got my sight back. I froze. The door opened and the woman who lived there looked me in the eye and I suppose you could say we stared each other down for a good minute."

Did David Livingstone recognize the woman?

"No. But she knew me."

Describe her.

"About my age. Glasses. Turquoise earrings. Jeans, a denim shirt. She wore a bandanna over her hair, purple. Her bandanna, not her hair. She had a mug in her hand, from some Universal Studios adventure tour. The coffee in it was still steaming, a hazelnutty aroma. I didn't see the inside of her house, but I remember thinking that it smelled of bread, and I could hear a whirring which made me think of our bread machine at home. And I think it was about then that she threw that mug in my face. It bounced off my forehead and the coffee slopped all the way down my front."

He did not remember the woman coming at him with her fists, much less her name. he did not recall what had transpired in between the moment when he found himself running at top speed down the street and the moment he registered the need for his hurry: the forest green Subaru Outback barreling behind him. He swore, in court and before his Maker, if it came to that, that the front bumper of her vehicle touched the backs of his shins once. It was at that point that he resorted to sprinting in a zig-zag, across and in loops, one side of the street to the other, which caused the woman in the Subaru to momentarily lose control of the wheel and make a perfect spin at the intersection, where a minivan at the stop sign honked and a girl on a skateboard fell into a flaming bird of paradise and cursed, scattering red and orange petals. He took this opportunity to cut through the backyards, knowing that, as the crow flies, this route would bring him directly from Lower Albert Road to Lupercal Path.

"I lost her," he pointed out.

Emerging from Lupercal Path to his own address, perspiring, heaving, scratched, shedding leaves, he was stunned at the quiet, the hum in the air indicative of automatic technology, sprinklers going on at two-thirty, garage doors opening and shutting at the master's approaching car. His surroundings were verdant and still. He might have said tranquil, though he looked this way and that for a forest green Subaru.

He saw one, noted a purple bandanna, and ducked into his own rosemary bush. The offending car whined when it stopped, not at his house, but at the so-called little library on the corner across the way. Quaint, cozy, it had the look of an overlarge birdhouse, painted yellow and fixed with a glass door so that you could see what was in there, as well as a small clipboard and a pen to record what had been taken out. It was put in by the neighborhood association last year, for the children, but really, David Livingstone suspected, as a method of getting rid of sticky chapter and picture books. His wife, against his wishes, supplied the little library with his girls' copies of *Ramona Quimby* and *Frog & Toad*. He could see them, squeezed among the Richard Scarrys, the Berenstain Bears, and the Harry Potters, just as well as he could see the woman in the purple bandanna get out of her car to plant more, as though that was what she'd come this way to do all along.

The fruit on the trees here could not be picked unless you had been invited to eat of it.

Blessed are You, Lord our God, King of the Universe, who creates the fruit of the tree. No one had ever made such a blessing over bland pears and hard-as-rock peaches fertilized by Home Depot mulch in their lives.

As for David Livingstone, he would not say where he lived or how closely he lived to Lower Albert Road. He waited in the rosemary. He came to doubt, even as he saw the purple bandanna and the Subaru and felt, in addition, the graze from its bumper on the backs of his shins, that the incident had happened. He reasoned. He had faith. He saw the two as interchangeable. He questioned if the blindness (if it wasn't too much to call it that) came about as the result of something that could be measured—stress, say, over his daughter's return and her condition. At almost thirty, she refused to bathe and, though she complied with the diapers, shrugged at stepping into them, knowing that she would just as quickly step out of them again to relieve herself in the backyard, as the dog did. His wife had all but washed her hands of her, in the figurative as well as the literal, considering the cleanup. He nor she had not expected to revisit the potty-training years with their own children.

He bristled, thinking of his wife's outburst only that morning, on her knees to scrub an offending dark patch on the living room's blue carpet: "It's not as if she's handicapped. She knows goddamned well what she's doing."

But, returning to the episode of blindness, however profound, however thankfully brief it was, he suspected that, if he were to go to a doctor for a full examination, he and the physician would both find all aspects of the orb, the retinas, the portion of the brain that they were attached to, to be thoroughly intact. David Livingstone had listened to the Who's *Tommy* growing up, wearing out the record, and listened to it now, wearing out the CD. He'd caught *The Story of Esther Costello* on Turner Classic Movies, having heard of it but never having seen it while it was first in theaters. Both, more or less, had the same plot: a traumatized young person is rendered deafblind and mute and emerges from their darkness and silence through some strength of will. A religious following occurs, it is seen as a miracle. David Livingstone concurred that the same was true of himself, here and now, though he suspected that such cases were more common than rock and roll and Hollywood would want anyone to believe.

The Subaru disappeared. The woman had come to do her errand, and that was that. He decided that she had not chased him, just as he decided that the blindness had been psychosomatic, which was also to say that it was all in his imagination.

He emerged from the rosemary, fragrant and stuck all over with splinters. He brushed down his clothes. He'd been about to go in when he caught sight first of four paws that ambled along the house's gutter. They gripped its edge by their long toes, and he was momentarily beguiled by their unfaltering, sweeping unity, each pink pair doing exactly what it was designed to do, one side followed with grace by the other, never afraid of miscalculating or mis-stepping. It was not arrogance. It was not showing off. It was what you would do if you had prehensile feet and toes like fingers. You would be more assured of your own abilities, wouldn't you?

David Livingstone told his daughter to come down. She perched on the gutter's edge and watched him. She did not speak, but it was clear that she wanted to know why she could not be on the roof. In her hoarse voice, she told him that she'd been sleeping up there.

Her father asked, "What's the matter with your bed? Or the couch?"

She said, "I don't like it."

He said, "Come down."

She said, "Not right now."

He pronounced, "No roof."

She repeated, "Not right now. Later."

He barked, "No. Now. No roof."

She clarified, "I like it here."

He growled, "No roof. Now."

"And then she looked at me," he said, after that time and these events had passed, "as though I was the presumptuous one. She, from, I suppose, her elevated point of observation, squatting there on my gutter, on my house, on my property—I don't know if I told you, but there was an odor, I think, coming from up there on the roof. I'm sure she went to the restroom up there." His wrath refreshed, he began again, "On my house, on my property. On my house—" This he repeated with breathless outrage, as though in response to a great sacrilege, the vandalizing of a temple. "She had the nerve to ask me who I thought I was." And again, raising his voice, "SHE asked ME."

David Livingstone went quiet. The silence did well to clear his mind. He echoed his daughter's words, which were less of an inquiry, now that he had to think of it, and more of a declaration. "Who do you think you are." He said it without the proper inflection, indicative of a question. "She's not wrong. Who do I think I am. Who do I think I am, while she's been in the garden all this time. The garden where she was invited, and left of her own volition. I'm just a poor imitation, I guess, of the real deal."

His own yard was trimmed and mulched. His wife's flowers, orange and red birds of paradise, the rosy crepe myrtle, the bleeding hearts and the day lilies and the columbines and the Dutch tulips and the one persimmon tree that yielded fat black, pebble-sized fruits that were edible, it seemed, for no more than twenty-four hours, the ivy they'd trained to climb its stump and snake along the arbor and up to the gutter where his daughter, who was not yet human in the way that apes and children are not yet human, cast her judgement, where she had (upon her father's later discovery, when he was up there scraping old leaves from the roof), in fact, relieved her bowels.

He had gotten a glimpse of the real deal. He'd decided that to talk too much about it would be blasphemous or, at least, an invitation for the blindness to return.

Then, as he'd done when he decided that his near running-down by the woman in the Subaru was imagined, he recalled that his neighbor across the way had been playing the radio. Across the way, the neighbor had a set of free weights in his garage, where he liked to lift with the door raised, music on, his exercise open to the public, a performance.

David Livingstone said, "He'd been listening to that Gnarls Barkley song. There's a part where he sings, *Who do you think you are?* She said it at the same time, she was pitch perfect. It's a popular song."

His two remaining daughters were expected that night. When asked if he thought it would have been wise to reintroduce them, David Livingstone said, "What happened happened. You can't predict who will influence who. And you can't pin it on me."

Allred Avery-McKnight became less articulate over the following days. He also slept less, but when he did, torpor struck suddenly and without regard to time or place. It began when his mother brought him along on a day of errands and, while waiting in line at the pharmacy, she turned to ask if he wanted a Sprite from the coolers and found him deeply asleep, albeit standing upright, his head bent to his chest. As Allred could not be woken and could not be persuaded to walk, even as a somnambulist, the strong fellow behind them and a very fit pharmacist had to rock him on his feet to make him fall into the arms of the former while the latter caught his ankles, and the two carried him out to his mother's car in that way.

Fourteen hours later, when he woke, he told his parents that he wanted to go home.

His stepfather assured Allred that he was home, that his mother had driven and here he was.

Allred shook his head and repeated what he'd said before, slower now, for emphasis.

His mother suggested that he must have had a bad dream. After all, he had been out for a little more than half a day.

Still, Allred said, "I want to go home."

He was settled in the room which had been his many years ago and was now made up for guests. Artifacts from his childhood, including his grade school sticker books, had been unearthed and brought up from the basement, perhaps in an effort to jog his memory, his humanity. His stepfather added to his stepson's music collection. While Joel McKnight was not proficient with modern variants of mp3 players and did not trust the payment scheme of iTunes, he managed to burn a twelve-track CD, beginning with Earth, Wind, and Fire's "Devotion" and ending with Gnarls Barkley's "Crazy". He thought Allred seemed pleased with it, for the younger man never went without the CD player. They were mostly songs from the older man's younger days, if not his youth, Todd Rundgren's "Change Myself" invoking a family reunion in Colorado, Phil Collins' "I Can't Stop Loving

You" his wedding reception and, by extension, Allred's kindergarten graduation. Allred listened and occupied the single bed. The sheets were green flannel. The pillowcase had Yogi Bear on it.

He occupied the single bed, though he managed to sleep in it for maybe an hour or two throughout the night. From a small hour until seven o'clock when his parents rose, Allred toddled about the house. He remembered very little of it, his mother suspected, thinking that, because it had been a new house when he disappeared, there was no reason for him to be very attached to it now. "We had only moved in about eighteen months before," Donna Avery-McKnight said. She would often discover her son at the kitchen table, either seated in one of the chairs with one leg or both wrapped around its back or perched on the cushioned edge, not eating, not reading anything, very still in his bizarre poise, like a lizard.

"He would tell me the time," Donna added. "I don't know if he was doing that to let me know that this was something he remembered from before, how to tell time."

"It's seven-o-four," he would say.

"It's six-fifty-three," he would say.

"Why do you get up at that hour?" he would ask.

It was a reasonable question. Joel and Donna were both retired, Joel semi. He went in as needed these days, and never before nine. They supplied an answer that ought to have satisfied but nevertheless mystified him, that it was a good hour to rise.

Donna told him, "You used to be the first one up, yourself."

Donna reminisced, "We could hear him at five or six in the morning, jumping around his room, music on. We had to beg him to rest for another hour."

Allred recounted some of his routine during his absence. He woke when the others did. They woke shortly before dawn. They bathed in the river and ate from the trees. The weather was never anything less than fine, even when it rained.

"So, it did rain?" Joel asked him.

"Yes," said Allred.

"There was daytime and nighttime?"

"Yes."

"Were there seasons? Do you remember the temperature dropping or rising? Did you have snow or ice or sleet where you were?"

"No."

Joel asked, "So, it was sunshine all the time?"

Allred blinked. "No. There was rain."

"You said there was a river. When it rained, did the river ever flood?"

"No."

"I suppose it never dried out either?"

"No."

"What kind of things did you eat from the trees?" the GP asked.

"Fruit," Allred told him at his next appointment.

"Like apples, oranges? Things like that?"

"I don't know."

"You know what oranges and apples look like." The GP showed him, having brought one of each to accompany his Tupperware of soup at lunch. The apple was an overlarge Granny Smith, the orange without fragrance and leathery around the outside. "Like these."

The patient shook his head. "Those aren't fruit."

"Sure, they are. You can eat them, you've been eating them."

The GP had it from the patient's mother that her son had been eating steadily, if without relish, since his return. He understood that whatever she put on his plate would nourish him, and, drawing from memories of his varied preferences from the age of nine going backward, she fixed dishes that she recalled having been successes. His tastes then had been, as she described, "all over the map", having enjoyed Annie's macaroni and cheese until something unknown to her but glaring to him had changed about the recipe, or Claussen pickles until he decided that he simply no longer cared for them or for any other brand of pickle. She knew that there were old favorites, her mother's black bean soup recipe that was so well-liked she had published it in the local newspaper, Shake 'n' Bake chicken, Stovetop cornbread stuffing, HEB brand couscous and wild rice, frozen peas cooked with butter and dill and black pepper and garlic salt, steamed broccoli florets and Ken's ranch dressing.

"He ate them now the way you might consume fuel. Or, I guess, an MRE," Joel put in. "I think it was mostly to please us. We'd been concerned— particularly since this business about not being able to see, hear, or smell. His main concern, he kept saying, was not being able to smell anymore, and we worried that perhaps this was the genuine—maybe this was affecting his ability to eat at first, when he first came home."

The patient understood that he was a foreigner among foreigners and that customs differed. He had said as much, in these words. He demonstrated this by using silverware, though his mind appeared to battle other instincts. His mother described the act of using a knife and fork as something that inspired great caution in her son, in the way one would exercise such caution before handling a chainsaw. He approached them as though he did not trust himself with them; he managed to cut small slivers from his meat before placing the utensils, politely but fearfully, at the far end of his plate. His natural inclination was to eat with his fingers, which he did, until his parents insisted that he give the knife and fork another try.

"Are you afraid you might hurt yourself with them?" his mother asked.

"I don't know," he said.

There was another question she thought of

posing. She could not bring herself to put it into words, to ask, "Are you afraid you might hurt us?" She did not want to have to reconsider familiar objects, a fork as a weapon.

Instead, she told him, "They're both very blunt." She showed him the fork prongs, the rounded edge of the butter knife. "They can't cut you."

Allred said, "Yes."

"You know it doesn't look nice, eating with your hands like that."

Her son listed the things he had observed others eating with their hands and that he himself had brooked no issue when he ate with his hands: Sushi, French fries, Klondike bars, mixed nuts. His mother acknowledged that, while this was true, there were expectations when it came to certain foods, especially if you were sitting down to eat, in particular with company.

"I ate with company before," he said.

"I want to go home," he said.

Because this house had not truly been home at the time of his going, his parents obliged what they hoped to be the triggering of an earlier memory, of what they had and continued to call the Old House. The Old House was roughly a forty-five-minute drive from where they lived now, where they had first congregated as a family unit. It had been Joel's home when he and Donna married. Allred had been four at the time, having lived in two different apartments and, prior to that, his grandmother's house. His mother asked him once if he meant the house he and his mother had lived in before the apartments, before his grandmother's house.

"No," he said.

Had he meant one of the apartments? One had a pool. The other had a dog park and a jungle gym.

"No," he said.

Had he meant his grandmother's house? She asked again. His grandmother had passed six or seven years into his absence, and he remembered less of her than her home. At any rate, his answer was a firm, "No."

Without posing the question, his parents concluded that the home he missed was the place they made the forty-five-minute sojourn to one weekend, when the weather was fine and weekend traffic tame. Joel put on Steely Dan, "Reelin' in the Years", "Rose Darlin'", citing them as perfect driving music, noting, too, how much Allred had liked them. They were among the musicians Joel had included on the mixed CD. The route took the family through a series of country towns whose revenue seemed to be generated through wineries, apple orchards, art galleries, and places where you could get a great sandwich, an unbelievable salad. They stopped at one such spot, on the corner of a main drag, which was in between a pottery shop and an old mill that had been reappropriated as a children's museum. The children's museum had a huge mechanical hand in their courtyard, with fingers that could be manipulated by a button-and-joystick keyboard installed in the lobby. Someone was working the hand to make it do a peace sign, a live-long-and-prosper-salute, and when the hand folded itself into flipping the bird to all and sundry, a manager rushed into the courtyard and fixed an Out of Order message to the mechanism's base. It took another ten or twenty minutes to get the hand to unlock and unfold again. The McKnights watched from a sidewalk patio. Joel had a great BLT, Allred and his mother unbelievable southwest salads with house-made chipotle ranch. Allred pushed his silverware to the edge of the table and ate with his hands. He worked with care, though it was a crisis to keep his mouth closed. He spilled dressing down his chin.

"Jesus Christ," his mother sighed.

"Don't do that," his stepfather snapped, making his wife think that he was talking about her and leading to a period of sullenness that lasted until they pulled up to a house that none of their party remembered very well. It had not been the house that Donna Avery-McKnight had grown up in. It was a place to which her mother had resigned herself, following a collapse in her former, two-story home in another state. Everything in this neighborhood was ground floor, retirement homes. There were small dogs, and children were an intermittent presence.

There was only one basketball hoop amid signs for home surveillance. There were thick, breathing trees and a service that came in the fall to rake the leaves. Joel visited here but once or twice before his mother-in-law's passing. Allred, who did not remember it at all, asked why he had lived here.

"Because Mam-Maw was getting sick," his mother said, "and we—"

"Who's that?"

"Your grandmother."

"Who are you?"

"I am your mother."

It was a conversation they'd had more than once, a recent development. His parents worried for their son's memory. While he seemed to recognize that there was a connection, if not a bond, between them, he had in a matter of days lost track of what exactly that connection was. Their fixture as mother and stepfather, as well as that broad linkage of grandparents and other relations, was an agnostic one. He was suspicious of it, not believing. His mother had theories; he must think of them as impostors, he must think of them as holograms. Her son was crazy, and people who were crazy thought along these lines. His mother hazarded a guess that he looked disappointed. She admitted later that she told him so, that day.

"Don't look so disappointed," were her words.

"I'm not," were her son's.

"Stop," was Joel's and all was still. No one moved from the car.

No one moved from the car because Joel had an idea. The idea came from his observation that the street, which was otherwise quiet and straight, ended in a sudden hump after you passed through the first stop sign. It was not quite a hill, though if you gave your car enough speed going up, you could easily get your vehicle about a foot in the air. The neighborhood they went to after they'd moved out of Allred's grandmother's house had a hump in the road just like it. The thrill was akin to a low-impact rollercoaster. Allred had loved it, according to Joel. According to Joel, Allred would pester him to "do the hill". On the way to school, on the way home, the Ford Taurus Joel then drove and no one else around.

"Please, can we do the hill?" Joel had the words crystallized in his memory. "I told him it was probably bad for the transmission. But he did say, Please can we do the hill."

Donna said, "Joel did the hill once and Allred loved it. And every time Joel was behind the wheel, we'd do the hill. It freaked me out, I'm not the kind of person who does the rides at Six Flags. And I would never rev the car up like that."

Now, twenty years later, Joel put the car into drive, peered over the steering wheel at the minor incline, turned, and said, "Let's do the hill." The neighborhood was not theirs, and unfamiliar to Joel.

There was no one else around. A thousand years ago, his son sat in place of the ape that occupied it now, his articulation and enthusiasm tokens of the promise that this child would evolve into a being that was fully human, one of his and his wife's shaping. What did that say about them, that this child had grown, but into something just this side of recognizable? What did it say, when the child, who had not fallen victim to the ordinary horror of breaking-and-entering, of molesters and kidnappers, had instead chosen to leave? Had chosen to leave and wanted to go home. He had chosen to leave and wanted to go home, and what did that say about their efforts as his sculptors? They were not God, but they were earthly representatives. Clay was only as good the hands it fell into. They had worked with care. They had not made this.

Joel turned in his seat and said, "Let's do the hill."

Donna nodded and acquiesced to her own sudden merriment. "I said wouldn't it be fun. I asked Al if he remembered. Joel asked Al if he remembered. Al shook his head."

"Sure, you do," Joel said, and the car barreled ahead.

Allred gripped the back of the passenger seat. His mother patted one paw, determined not to recoil at the fur, though now spare, that came off onto her fingers. She told her son that he remembered this. He insisted that he did not.

The speed limit in a residential area is typically

thirty miles per hour. Joel took the vehicle to forty, then fifty, then, with the confidence that there really was no one else around, seventy. His wife whooped. The stereo played Steely Dan, "Reelin' in the Years" and "Rose Darlin'". There was the structure of a rollicking good time. It was fall and the neighborhood was a blur, orange and yellow overwhelming the green. You were supposed to lose yourself at times like these. You were supposed to put everything to rest, your age and your job and your circumstance, and just let go.

Allred whimpered. His fingers, the appendages long and the nails black and the knuckles thick, changed their place and were now tight on his mother's shoulders. The fur on them was as pubic hair, wiry and prone to matting. Bits of lunch were caught in it. You could imagine those hands taking apart a face as readily as a southwestern salad.

Donna told him to let go.

He would not.

"That made him more upset," she later said. "I tried prying him off. He kept scrabbling for me. He wouldn't so much as hug me before."

Donna told her son to enjoy himself. She did not want to be repulsed. Her words, in truth, were, "We're having fun. So have fun, goddammit."

Allred wept. He said, "I want to go home."

Joel, looking shamefaced, said, "He jumped out of the car after I went around the cul-de-sac a second time. I was channeling *The Truman Show*, the part where Jim Carrey speeds around the cul-de-sac in his neighborhood."

His wife said, "In retrospect, that we didn't flip the car. That there wasn't a cop in the area. I don't know how fast we were going, but it wasn't thirty miles per hour. That Al could judge the right time to do what he did and keep running—and come away from this with a mild sprain—"

What Allred Avery-McKnight did was leap from the vehicle to the island at the cul-de-sac's center. He perched on the memorial boulder, still for a moment, too quickly for his parents to witness as they struggled to regain control of the car. Using the boulder as a platform, he leapt again, one foot and one paw hitting the vehicle's roof before he sped down the sidewalk in a four-limbed sprint. The street was otherwise quiet, empty, despite the agreement all around of what a fine day it was. There was no one to see the creature in jeans and a blue L.L. Bean polar tech lope in a fright toward their homes.

"My mother's house was not occupied at the time," Donna Avery-McKnight said. "It was closed. It went through a few different owners since we'd been there, and that day there was a realtor's sign out front. I'd already checked the listings, just out of curiosity, and it was on the market. We caught up with him just in time to catch him going up one of the posts on the front porch. We stood out front and called. He turned and told us again that he wanted to go home. And he pounded on the two upstairs windows for a good minute or so. Then it seemed that he had a moment of clarity, like he remembered how windows worked, and he tried pushing at the frames, to see if either window was open. They weren't, of course. Everything was locked. Barring that, he went back to pounding and scraping—I was appalled. I was really very frightened."

Not at the noise, not at the creature. Instead, Donna took in the silence. All was still this day. Not a soul emerged from the houses to investigate. No curtains stirred, and she was convinced that the neighborhood in its entirety had been deserted. It would be very likely, she felt, that she could peer through any picture window and find bare living rooms, pristine as the day they were finished, untouched by human tenants, like an episode of *The Twilight Zone.* She could bang on every door, and she decided at the last minute that it might be worse, in fact, if someone were to answer. She had already determined that the homes were vacant without having to snoop. An occupant, she reasoned, would be a harbinger of bad news. She imagined something blandly nightmarish, a demon coming to the door in the guise of a smiling local, coffee mug in hand, just through from the garden out back, perfectly benign, here to tell her that her son was doomed.

Filled with spiteful urges, misdirected as they

were at imagined foes, Donna recalled herself shouting at the blank windows. She did not recall what was said, though she speculated that it was along the lines of "Fuck you, too." Whatever was said was magnified by the quiet, and she was taken aback at the clarity of her own voice bouncing from garage door to garage door before landing squarely at its point of origin. It hit her in the chest, she said.

Turning back to her mother's house, hearing as if for the first time her husband's voice and, at last, allowing him to guide her, pull her by the elbow, toward the yard, she found that her son had exhausted all civilized methods of breaking in through the window and had smashed the glass with first the flats of his paws, then his head. This was according to Joel.

"I could not go inside," Donna said. "I could not go to any door. I was frozen where I was. I had my husband do it."

Joel went first to the next-door neighbors' homes, to the left and to the right, to see if they had a spare key in their possession, but there was no one there. After an interlude in which he was obliged to comfort his wife, in which both found themselves quietly cursing and weeping on the curb, it was she who summoned the wherewithal to call the local police's non-emergency number. When they arrived, in a single car occupied by two benign-looking officers, the party found a back door that had never been locked by the previous tenants and entered through the kitchen.

"Allred had already been in there," Donna said. "We could see footprints on the floor. He'd come downstairs. He'd taken off his shoes."

He'd thrown his shoes down the stairs before descending. The search party found them in the foyer, a pair of black Vans slip-ons, as he'd lost the ability to cope with laces and knots. There had been some mild flooding in the foyer during the rainy winter, and its tiled floor was slightly damp underfoot. It was the damp that yielded a trail of breadcrumbs, that is, faint impressions of Allred Avery-McKnight's feet. Police and parents traced them through the empty rooms, and they were briefly confused by their number and how quickly the young man had gone from top to bottom floor, from foyer to kitchen to bathroom to living room to sunroom in so little time, and, it seemed, so thoroughly.

Donna said, "It looked like the diagram of feet you see in a dancing book. How to do the foxtrot, I don't know. But they were everywhere."

So they were, and the markings were distinct in the splaying of the toes and their length, seeming to have grown even in the few minutes since their son had vanished for the second time. The electricity was out, and the officers were happy to make use of their police-issue flashlights. They were also happy to allow the couple to conduct the lion's share of the search while they trailed far behind. They asked if their son was unwell.

"I didn't know how to answer that," Donna said, "I went on upstairs and pretended I hadn't heard."

"They caught me coming up from the cellar," Joel said, "I had no choice but to say that, yes, yes, Al was unwell."

"I didn't want to say that he was unwell because —" Donna paused to reconsider the why and the wherefore. "—because I'm not sure if he was."

The officers asked if their son was experiencing a psychotic episode. They asked if he had been experiencing hallucinations, if he had been assigning importance to things that would otherwise have no meaning. Joel called their GP on his mobile number and when he could not be reached there, at his home.

Donna, meanwhile, continued the farce of not having heard and extended the play into not having seen the fresher, larger, wetter prints that led up to and abruptly stopped at the window, not the broken one, of the third and smallest bedroom. This had been Allred's room during the year or so of their time here. It looked out into the tiny backyard and into the yard of the people behind them, and of the people behind them, and so on until the highway. Donna compared the panorama of houses and yards to gazing into an infinity mirror, wherein the twinned reflections seem to go on forever. She knew that the neighborhood, though tidy, was not full. She knew, without having to read up on the current real estate situation, that less than half of these houses were, true to her recent horror, quite empty. She wondered what that might mean. She wondered if the horror did not so much lie in the blankness, the indifference, after all, so much as the stillness. This was not her home, what prevented her from having entered? Not the police. It had been easy to trespass, and she hadn't needed to show so much as a driver's license. It made her think, instead of her son, of what all she might have gotten away with in her spryer and younger days, by virtue of what? Her eloquence? Her large eyes? Her ability to cry at the drop of a hat? This was not to say that she was now or ever had entertained fantasies of a life of crime. What she considered, really, was detachment—from the law, from convention, from boundary.

Look at that window, she wanted to tell Joel. Passing from this room (which bore no trace of her mother's chinoiserie wallpaper) to the next (which, for whatever reason, still had it), she beheld the window that her son had put his hand or his head through. She could see that, while Allred could no longer cope with shoelaces, he could work out how to operate a latch, and had slipped in that way. It was still bright where he'd cut himself, and the pawprint smack in the middle of cavorting cranes and chrysanthemums was a rude testament to his presence there, what he'd been before, what he'd become, what he'd left once and would leave again.

Had left again.

Detachment. Donna envied him for it, and it was instantaneous and enveloping. Was that all you would have to do? Imagine salvation that easily got. Instead of taking up a cross and following the first one who called themselves the way and the light, was it only required that you take off your shoes? And once you'd done that, the rest of your apparel? And once you'd shed that, all industry and ambition? And once you'd renounced that, speech? Might something magical occur, as it surely had with this select few, her son a blessed one of them? It was possible to become something else, if you put your mind to it. How often had she seen it achieved by Allred himself, a crusty, squealing three-year-old that had to be reprimanded for shitting in the McDonald's ball pit into a soaring performer that could stop and start on a dime--a mini Robin Williams, she'd called him-- seemingly within a matter of minutes? When you are a child, years are as moments. Transformations can be quick and also permanent.

What were some of the things she used to say?

"You have to want it."

"You have to put in some real effort."

"You have to make a commitment."

"You have to get it together."

Because one time he'd said something offhand? Vaguely looking at the TV when this room had been Donna's and they'd been watching *Mrs. Doubtfire* and he announced that he'd like to do what Robin Williams did when he grew up?

Well, in her defense, he had wanted it.

"I think it was maybe a year later he was getting roles in plays at the community theater," Donna said, "And already so polished."

She remembered the TV being right around where his pawprint was now. She followed the prints back into the smallest bedroom, where she stopped, stooped, caught her breath.

Allred was here, though not as he had been in these new days. He appeared to not have left this house at all, as though the memory had been enough to preserve him just as he was. If she had to guess, Donna would have put him at about three years old. He looked just as capable of shitting in any public place, let alone a McDonald's ball pit. He was clothed only in the t-shirt he'd put on that morning, evergreen cotton from the men's section at L.L. Bean. Now he bore it up like a Roman toga, with the hem skimming below his knees. The cotton was filthy, as though he'd been rutting in dirt for all of his natural life with but this shirt to block him and the muck. There was a healing wound at his hairline that reached the top of his scalp—where he had banged his head to get in, Donna thought--and puffy pink scarring on the tiny ham of his toddler's paw. He still looked dazed, less frightened, though Donna knew that if she were to move too quickly or to speak too loudly that it would all come back and he would be gone again.

Donna said, "So I sat on the floor."

Donna said, "I asked him what had happened to the rest of his clothes."

Donna said, "His teeth were so tiny. He hadn't even lost his baby teeth yet. I wanted to touch his hair because I knew how soft it would be, once we'd washed him. God, he was caked in mud. And dust. He didn't look underfed or dehydrated or anything. He didn't look unwell."

Allred, much smaller, unfurred, much more pitiable, said, "I don't like them." Then he hugged himself. "I like just this." He gripped with his baby monkey's hands the shoulders of the t-shirt that now swamped him. The sleeves flapped around his elbows like ceremonial robes. It made his mother think of Mickey Mouse in *The Sorcerer's Apprentice*.

Joel, when he came upstairs, and the police officers, when they followed, did not know what to make of this dirty little boy, each party in their own way: Joel astonished at the shedding of years in his stepson that had occurred in no more than an hour, the officers baffled at all the fuss that was taking place over, what amounted to them, a temper tantrum.

"One of them said," Joel later seethed with Donna as his second in their brooding, "that we should've told them our son was just a kid. They asked if Al was armed. I said I didn't know. They were making arrangements for backup, in case he had a weapon. They asked if he was a danger to himself or others. I said I didn't know, only that he was unwell. I couldn't tell them the rest, of course. Certainly not after going upstairs and finding him this way."

The officers knelt to give Allred a benignly stern lecture about running away before rising to cut glances at Donna and Joel. Amused, suspicious or otherwise, the parents could not read countenances, save for each other's, which were masks of fury. Allred allowed them to pull Joel's polar tech over his head and to take him by both hands from the house. They knew that they had to be gentler with him, now that he was a child. They resisted the urge to physically lift him, just as he resisted any more contact than there had to be. Before his disappearance twenty years ago, he had submitted to kisses and hugs, whether he had wanted them or not. In this apparent second chance at youth, it was clear that such things would be forbidden. He gave his mother a nasty eye as she tried to touch his hair.

"I felt as though he'd done it on purpose," Donna said. "I asked him when we put him in the car why he'd done what he did. He said he hadn't done anything and that he was still the same. Joel asked him about his eyesight and his hearing and his ability to smell. Al said that it was the same as before. Before he'd gone upstairs that day. He ought to have been very injured going in through the window like that.

We asked him if anything hurt, and he said no. We asked him if he was cold, he said no. He was not as frightened as before. He looked—upset. I want to say either angry or deeply disappointed. Deeply disappointed, as in, someone hoping for a certain result and not getting it. I can imagine. At this point, he was a little boy, perhaps entrenched in all the things you know as an adult. But he wasn't a normal adult, even when he was an adult."

As it happened, the Enamorados and the Livingstones woke to identical predicaments the following day.

Marisol said, "I went to see if Alonso was up yet. And he was. He was waiting for me as he was in the memories I have of him at four or five or six, always awake before me. When I went into his room, that's what I saw. My son at four or five or six, bundled up in the blankets because he was refusing to put on clothes. He followed me around the whole morning like that, with the blankets trailing behind like a cape. He had this very stony look, as though we were keeping him for some awful, unknown purpose. He never took his eyes off us. I think he knew that things had changed. I think he knew how vulnerable he was, now that he was back to a size where anybody could just pick him up and carry him off. It makes sense, when you're that small; everything is a menace. He'd stopped asking if we were going to kill him, but I didn't think it was wise to have my back turned to him when we were in the same room together. I didn't like how he was watching me."

David Livingstone said, "It was, I admit, much easier to attend to Jules, now that she was small again. By that, I mean it was easier to punish her. I came down to find her still sleeping in the dog's crate. She was deep asleep, and so I could ease the dog out of the crate and out to the backyard. And then I locked the crate. When she woke up, I told her that big girls don't sleep like dogs do, and when she was ready to act like a big girl, I would let her out." He elaborated, his voice trembling in order to make sense of the change and of his immediate turn of action. "She looked as she did when she was somewhere between ages three and six. That was around the age when she started to figure out how to pull strings, how to get her own way. My wife had complained about how manipulative she could be when she was young—before she went. And at the time, I hadn't listened. My wife thought that caging her was going too far. She told me that it was cruel. I asked her what she thought ought to be done and she left the room."

Marisol Enamorado, "I left him alone for only a minute or two. I pretended to need the bathroom to get away from him. I was relieved when he didn't follow me in, and the quiet in those sixty plus seconds was reassuring—I thought that, since he'd lived this part of his life before, that he'd have the wherewithal to handle being on his own. Maybe some things would return to him. Maybe whatever was clouding his mind would dissipate. I mean. I mean, he looked just the same as he did when he was a little boy. All that fur was gone—it was all over his mattress now, I don't know if it just fell out or if he'd been pulling it out. He stood upright like a person. Or I suppose it was easier now, because of his small size, to stand up straight. I think his arms had been a burden to him before, they were so long, and his shoulders had to bear the weight, so he was slumped over a lot of the time. But now everything was in proportion. The only thing that stayed the same were his feet, still like hands, though they were covered most of the time because of the blankets. Anyway. I thought he'd remember certain things that came with growing up. I was sitting on the toilet and thinking that maybe the worst was over now. I was on my own, you know. My husband wasn't well. He was having trouble remembering who was who, what year it was. I thought that this must be—as I was brought up to think, as I had been, until recently, wont to think— that this was God's work. The Lord restored our child from whatever he had been, wherever he'd been. Maybe this was our second chance. Hardly those words were out when I heard him screaming upstairs."

Mrs. Livingstone said, "I had to let her out. I had to let her out so that her sisters could see her. I still wanted to have the get-together. David was against it from the start, more adamantly now that she had changed again. Maybe he was afraid that she would shift halfway through the cookout into a full-blown gorilla. I think that was the point when I understood that, whatever was happening, whatever this was, there was no way to contain it. Jules was Jules, and this was between her and something quite beyond our ken. It was as though whatever furtive prayers we had were considered from on high and answered. And if that's so, I would say that He who answered had a very 'Be careful what you wish for' kind of attitude. If I've learned anything from this, it's that God is a real prankster."

Marisol Enamorado said, "I ran into his room and he was sitting in the middle of his bed with his top two teeth in his hand. He was hysterical. And I made it worse. I just stood there and said something like, 'Oh, is that all?' Because he'd been through this before. I think the first time he lost a baby tooth was in kindergarten. It was his bottom front teeth then, both at the same time, while he was eating a nectarine. That was a fun day, and I think Alonso would've said the same. His teacher was a very nice lady, Mrs. Welsch or Mrs. Watts. Anyway, she let him show them to his class, and she put them in a plastic baggie to take home. I was a generous tooth fairy, I put a Dairy Queen coupon, plus a five-dollar bill under his pillow.

"I asked him to give the teeth to me, I'd wash them off. They looked like ordinary baby teeth. I had no reason to believe that another set wouldn't grow in. Which is to say that I could not. I tried to reassure him. All I knew to do was to repeat, over and over, 'You've been through this before. You're fine.' In retrospect, that must've been a very flippant thing to say. He couldn't get his breath, he was crying so hard. I tried to tell him about the tooth fairy. And that's when he came at me. He wanted his teeth back. But I do believe he meant to hurt me, too. I don't think he would've done much damage; I could lift him with one arm, and I did, over my shoulder. But, by golly, he put up a fight."

She paused, when asked, to show the scarring down her back. She reported that he'd bitten and scratched. She did not go to a doctor. As she said, with the same flippancy used in reference to her son's teeth, "He's not a werewolf. What was he going to do, turn me into one?"

Mrs. Livingstone said, when asked about God's place in these events, "It's disconfirmed, for me, something that I long convinced myself of and tried to dampen by telling myself, first and foremost, that old lament, that things that are unmanageable or unbelievable or scary or just flat-out weird only happen to other people. Car accidents, a run-in with an axe killer, an alien abduction, sudden onset schizophrenia, meningitis that eats up your limbs, kidnapping. The answer to that is this: We are other people. It's a rude shove, not really an awakening. You can't try and come up with a reason for this thing happening to you because you'll find a million of them, whether it was something you did twenty years ago or some little thing you said in jest. No idle word is forgotten, as the Good Book says. Another thing, one that I long suspected and tried to put out of my mind, is that I am an animal, too. I mean, we all are. That kind of puts a pall over this whole, shiny idea of being set apart from the apes and the gorillas, doesn't it? And I acknowledge that we are different. We sent folks to the moon. We figured out how to hack into people's bank accounts. Well. Whoop-de-do. Given enough time, I don't doubt that old idea that an ape can not only pound out Shakespeare on a typewriter, that same ape can invent fifty new methods for the death penalty and good-sounding reasons for them, too. I mean, we had enough time, didn't we? Several million years, which are as a blink of God's eye, as they say? And here we are."

Did any of them, parents of these incorrigible, changeling children, believe in God?

All were silent to that question, whereas, at any point in time prior to these events, they might have answered with an apostle's YES. Their answers, while still in the affirmative, were by turns wavering, whispered, weary. The Livingstone's daughter had used the word *nonbeliever*, one of the few words that she was willing (or able) to articulate. The Avery-McKnights and the Enamorados were not accused as such by their sons, though distrust from Allred and Alonso was marked. All three had been witness to a being known only in tales, and for their parents, to acknowledge its presence brought an unwelcome mixture of feelings. Mrs. Livingstone, as with Julian, began referring to her Maker as the creature, for it, too, had shown itself to be incorrigible and shifting, never mind that she had not seen or heard it. David Livingstone did not speak of it at all. Marisol Enamorado, once devout, had been at first keen to denounce these events as the work of the devil. Joel McKnight was in agreement with this sentiment, while his wife was not.

Donna Avery-McKnight said, "I think this is what we get for trying to fix God into one shape. I think this is what we get for doing the same to Al. It made everything so easy when Al was younger. We used to go to church. We were Episcopalian, we went to St. Steve's and that's where we got married. We had both been raised Catholic, and this felt like it was the gentler version—I think Robin Williams called it Catholic Lite. Anyway, fundamentally, it's not much different from anywhere else, in that, everything is of an order. There's cause and effect. There's a chain of action. You know that you were made and you know that you can be wiped out at any time. You don't question that. You don't even think about it. You just hope that things get better or that it's all over with soon. That's what most people pray for, you know. Let it get better or let it be over soon. You can't tell your kid that. Instead, you hope that the idea of God as a strict chain of action will be enough to keep him out of trouble. You hope that the Lord is a kindly old fellow, like Gandalf or something, if he had to show himself."

What did Donna Avery-McKnight think of God now?

"Not a being. Maybe a yearning."

Had Donna Avery-McKnight ever yearned for God?

"No. I never thought my son would yearn. I thought he would want for nothing."

Marisol Enamorado would not answer questions regarding the parents of the three children who were still missing. She had not sought them out twenty years before, at the time of their first disappearance. She said, "They exactly reach out to us either, you know." Nor did she seek them out now. She said, "Why? It might have reignited all that trauma from before. And they might have seen it as gloating, if we were to just call them up and tell them that Alonso was back. How might they have felt if they knew that Alonso was back and their kid wasn't? I could just give them a confirmation of death. And that's not my place. If they were going to come back, they would have come back. And anyway, we didn't know those people."

Others might have contacted the media, if their

missing child, after decades of unknowing, appeared in their home.

David Livingstone asked if anyone in his right mind would have thought it prudent to attract a swarm of reporters to a situation that was not only delicate but also very much a private one. Julian Livingstone's photograph was briefly featured on national news. Her image had been, while not exactly on milk cartons, then familiar enough to draw a stranger's eye and mind, enough to inspire that same stranger to say in passing, "Where do I know her from?" Whether the public knew that Julian Livingstone was alive and well was nobody's concern but that of the Livingstone family.

Mr. Enamorado whispered, when he was alone, "We shouldn't have brought him to church. That was a mistake. No one should've known about him. It would've been better if he'd stayed dead."

But Alonso Enamorado was not dead. He had been alive and he was alive, and he determined to remain so. He was filled, now that he as a child again, with a sense of urgency. His faculties, sharp before, were honed to their finest points, and it seemed to him that there was no truth that he could not perceive that his eyes, his ears, his nose, his nerves and his tongue could not catch. He had forgotten the years before, when his name and his species and his sex were said to be fixed. He knew that the missing years, those spent in the woods, had happened. They were as a dream to him in life, reconnecting at the provocation of a smell, a semitone, the look of light through leaves, and they returned to him in sleep.

Of the six who left their homes, he had been, in Donna Avery-McKnight's words, the one who yearned the most. He would not have called it God, despite knowing its function as such, as well as its separateness from himself. And its attachment. He knew that it was what lesser beasts knew and that this knowledge escaped his own species, for all its years of progress.

He remembered as clearly as though he were standing in that day, that moment, that day when his mother had had a dispute of some kind with the neighbor whose house backed up to theirs. Alonso had been nine. His mother had exchanged bitter words with the woman who had previously been relied upon for impromptu babysitting, laundry machine usage, the borrowing of birdseed. She was called Mrs. Baker or Mrs. Barker. Alonso had liked her well enough, and was puzzled that his mother could mine such rage from a mild accusation. Mrs. Baker or Mrs. Barker had seen or thought she'd seen Alonso's mother lifting coupons from her mailbox. It had begun when the neighbor went away on vacation and asked Marisol Enamorado to collect her mail for her. It was mostly junk, if Alonso's memory served him, catalogues and flyers and the disputed, coveted coupons. Upon her return, the neighbor knew she was meant to have or thought she was meant to have several items to discount store brand chips and salsa and two-for-ones on birdseed. Again, bitter words. Again, stink eyes from both parties. His mother told him that the neighbor had gone to New Mexico to dry out because she was an alcoholic. Whether or not this was true was very much of the unknown, though Marisol would repeat her claim to anyone who asked and who did not ask, that Mrs. Baker or Mrs. Barker was an alcoholic who was too plastered to know what she was talking about.

"You know why she went out to Santa Fe, don't you?" his mother would whisper, her voice husky, fiery, mornings after church services. "She's got a problem."

Alonso did not think that was true. His mother had never mentioned it before, and he thought she might have shown concern if the two were on good terms, if it was only performative. She brought it up every chance she got.

The neighbor's yard had been host to a variety of birds. She installed a birdbath surrounded by bells of Ireland, which looked to Alonso like stalks with large, friendly ears, and four birdfeeders, plus a hanging dish full of sugar water on the back porch for the hummingbirds. Throughout the seasons, he could count on the visitation of cardinals and oriels and doves, and more than once, the neighbor would show him, under some secrecy, how to stand still and just so, with his palm cupped and full of sugar water so that the hummingbirds would drink right out of his hand. She told him he had the look of Francis of Assisi.

Mrs. Baker or Mrs. Barker was a Catholic. His mother had never sniffed at the distinction, but since the argument, she grew keen to note the superstition and the suspicion and the overall witchery of the faith and its faithful. "I mean, you know what they're like, don't you?" she asked her son, who was not learned enough to tell the difference between a Catholic and a Calvinist. Indeed, he did not know what his own ecclesia called itself, save that they were right and everyone else was, very sadly, wrong.

He believed. He knew as much as that. He believed in the light through the leaves and the breath of fresh air and the birds that drank from his hand. It was a blessed contrast to the odors from cars. He knew that if he could have his way, if and when he grew up, he would move away and live far from anything foul. For he knew that he, too, was an animal.

It was around this time that the neighbor went away again, this time for an overnight trip. His mother had let up on the drying-out-in-New Mexico campaign. She had let up because she'd gone over the privacy fence with a pitcher of iodine and sugar and poured it into the birdbaths and the hanging dish on the neighbor's back porch. Twenty-four-hours later, there came a great cry from the neighbor's yard, and Alonso peered over the fence to join Mrs. Baker or Mrs. Barker in her mourning over the small, bright bodies of cardinals and oriels and doves and hummingbirds that lay like devalued gems in the grass. The neighbor sobbed as she fished them from the bottom of her in-ground pool.

He knew, too, that animals were hungry or frightened. They were never hateful.

He considered his mother's aptitude. He considered the ease with which she climbed over the fence. It might be nothing for her to do the same in her own domain, iodine in her son's cereal. For a while, until his vanishing, he refused to eat anything she prepared, and that included the store brand chips and salsa that she brought in at ten percent off, according to HEB receipts.

"You can't go around not eating," she told him.

"I'm not not eating," he said.

"All of a sudden, you're turning up your nose at what I put down in front of you."

"I ate at school."

"If you get too skinny, people will think we don't feed you."

"I'm not too skinny."

"Eat it."

"I don't want to."

He was unsure now if it was his mother who had snapped or his father who had had enough of the equally paranoid back-and-forth who finally shouted, "GODDAMMIT, JUST EAT IT." He did not recall what it was he'd had to eat, only that it was savory and steamy and something he'd liked.

For about a week after that, Alonso crept around the edges of the house. He was frightened at first, when, before he knew it, the fear had subsided completely and was infused with a familiar, very familiar, too familiar kind of glee, so much so that he took his sudden need to observe his mother in her most private moments of plucking her eyebrows and pulling out her tampons as a facet of his nature that was due to mature and solidify. To know where his mother was and what she was doing at any moment was necessary. He knew what for, though he did not understand it. Predators who are human often don't know where the urge comes from. His mother had never hurt him; this is another way of saying that his mother had not hurt him yet.

If she had no qualms about bearing false witness.

If she had no qualms about felling a flock of birds.

If she had no qualms about helping herself to coupons that did not belong to her.

Alonso wept, for he was full of a horrible knowledge that he could not shake. Up to this point, he had been content to go about his days as a lesser member of this unit, a step up from the elderly boxer-mix they'd then had. It was as though his parents had not quite grasped what it would mean to procreate.

And, looking around, he had to note that his situation did not much differ from that of other children's, in that, their time as a step up from the family pet was ending, that mothers and fathers in this neighborhood began to recognize (if not admit) that their offspring were more than mute absorbents for their own misdeeds. It is never comfortable to accept when you have done wrong, even privately. It must be, Alonso thought, unbearable when there are onlookers, especially when you have done the opposite of what you've told them to do.

Animals are hungry and frightened.

I am not hungry. Nor am I afraid. I should not want to do what I want to do.

He situated himself behind the drapes in the master bedroom. He wedged into the lowest shelf of the linen closet, which was also the widest, when he knew that his mother was going to use the bathroom. He stood directly behind her while she was busy at the computer, peeling cucumbers in the kitchen for a salad, or watching *Cosby Show* reruns on Nick at Nite. He would not breathe and she would not stir, and he wondered if she knew that she was no longer safe in her own house, as long as he lived in it.

He would disappear for the first time later that night and would not return for another twenty years. At which point, he would disappear again, this time for good. *The Cosby Show* would no longer be on television, even in reruns.

Julian knew a story that her father told her only once. It was about her grandfather, when he was sent to Germany during the second world war. Her mother, who had heard it many times over the course of her marriage, had not entirely believed it. She said of it, "I'm pretty dure David lifted it from a *Band of Brothers* episode."

According to David Livingstone, his father, accompanied by five fellow scouts from his platoon, entered the country home of a Nazi officer, looking for information. The officer refused to give it, citing loyalty to his nation and to the Fuhrer, and also unto God. The last angered Grandfather Livingstone to such a degree that he wanted to harm the officer beyond any scale that arrest, imprisonment, and torture had to offer.

It was an affront to his faith, in David's words. Though, more likely, it was an affront to what he knew his Maker to be. Just as it is never comfortable to accept when you have done wrong, it is all the worse when your very nature is reflected in another. You are keen to dismiss them. You make them into a cartoon. You echo that old idea like an incantation against a demonic intruder. You say, "I would never do that." Grandfather Livingstone knew that he had met his double, thousands of miles from where he started in life. It had taken a declaration of war to bring the two face to face.

As it happened, the officer was a father; his two small sons were just coming in from playing in the vineyards which surrounded the house. They looked to be about seven or eight or nine years old, and were barefoot. It was summer and this was the done thing for children in the German countryside, apparently, for there were no snakes to be found in the soft grass and the river (what the six soldiers would have called a creek) was warm and its waters shallow. At once, Grandfather Livingstone became bright, bountiful, an American who had Hershey rations in his pockets. The boys tore into them and trusted, their faces sweet and smeared brown. Grandfather Livingstone was said to have been terribly handsome in his heyday. There were six soldiers and there were five who stepped away from the boys and the Hershey bars; they did not want to deviate from routine procedure and had now, too late, found themselves in territory that was quite alien to them, despite its familiarity of a cool breeze and the smell of chocolate, a clear blue sky and a beaming star that was their sun. The officer's face quivered and it seemed that he had forgotten how to put words together, in English as well as in his own language.

They, all of them, were on another planet.

Grandfather Livingstone wanted to show the boys something outside, as soon as they'd finished with the Hershey bars. The boys balled the wrappers and threw them aside. They were sticky and obliging, running to the window where Grandfather Livingstone pointed. And, wouldn't you know, there was something out there worth looking at. The farm adjacent to the country house kept exotic animals, which by that time amounted to several peacocks and a large, grinning chimpanzee. The farmers had deserted and left the chimp to run things. By the time Grandfather Livingstone arrived to point it out, the chimp had gone mad by the abandonment and, in its agitation, plucked out patches of its own fur. When this was not enough, the chimp would bite and scratch itself, and it galloped on all fours around the complex with bald spots over its legs and ring-shaped wounds on its arms, looking infected. Now, bored with self-injury, it was in the flirtation stage of bullying the peacocks. Were it not for Grandfather Livingstone, it would surely have eaten them, but as it was, the chimp was only beginning to see the satisfaction that could be had from making them run to exhaustion, from plucking their feathers with its long fingers and gnashing its squared teeth and making them run again.

It was an awful scene and the boys laughed at it.

Grandfather Livingstone took this opportunity to put the barrel of his pistol to the back of one, then the other of the boys' heads. Following this, he shot the chimp, whose noise he could not bear, and when the officer's noises became a greater offense, Grandfather Livingstone shot him, too. He reasoned that it would have been cruel to leave him alive.

David Livingstone concluded the story thusly: "He meant the chimp."

Many years later, his eldest would pray to a God whom she had not, until now, believe in, to take her away.

I am not made to live in anger. I am not made to live in filth. I know that you have made a land of milk and honey. I know that it is written. And if you are what I think you are, you will bring me to that place to live without the burden of perversion. I am not of this species. If I am to crawl on all fours to find you, let it be. If I am to forsake all foulness, let it be.

Bring me home.

I am yours. I am an animal. I admit it. Bring me to that place.

It was twenty years ago that Mary Kathleen, Clare, Evander, Alonso, Allred, and Julian received the call from on high. Or, rather, from a deep sort of dream, in which a voice told them to wake, in softness and without language.

WAKE. UP.

Just like that.

WAKE. UP.

And, following that:

COME. HOME.

COME. HOME.

Like a telegraph.

COME. Stop. HOME. Stop. I. Stop. WILL. Stop. PROTECT. Stop. THEE.

They had all dreamed collectively, as children are wont to do. Children dream of losing teeth, permanent ones. They dream, too, of showing up at school in bunny pajamas—or, more embarrassingly, without one stitch of clothing.

On this night, twenty years ago, they dreamed of a God that kept its promises.

It whispered in a collective ear to WAKE.UP. and to COME. HOME.

Twenty years ago when they met in the enclosed circle of the park with the tennis courts and the municipal pool, they agreed that there was a place for them, far away from here. Three of them dreamed of an orangutang, large and orange and furred like a wizard. The other three dreamed of a gorilla, wide and solid and small-eyed.

When the parents heard of this, they knew not what to make of it, for God, to them, was not of them or among them, certainly not inclined to appear in dreams in the form of a great ape.

Mrs. Livingstone shook her head and said, "This sounds like something out of *2001*."

David Livingstone called it blasphemy, though he did not sound as convinced as he might have been.

Joel and Donna McKnight said nothing. They hung their heads, for they were deeply ashamed of what they had almost done to their son.

Their GP Paul said, "I believe it. I'm a Jew. I'm not particularly religious, but I am, by birth, consummately, ultimately, a Jew. I'm not kosher. I don't abide by every rule. But I believe in the importance of dreams. Every prophet dreamed. And I dreamed this when I was nine or ten years old, still in my trundle bed and knowing nothing. I dreamed that there was a being that loved me. Without constraints. Without conditions. And who would bring me home if things got to be too much. Who would prevent me from exiting this mortal coil by any means possible, even if I were to live in animal penury. I dreamed that I was called out of my bedroom. I climbed out, down the rose trellis, into the backyard. I could feel the chill on my bare feet, the cuffs of my hand-me-down jammies. I wandered through my neighborhood. The lights and the mailboxes and the parked cars and the sidewalks. There was a hopscotch grid etched, initials, flowers and bees and trees in cotton candy colors. I kept going. I kept going until the sidewalk disappeared out from under me, from under my feet. I heard music along the way from the passing vehicles, a lot of Steely Dan. *Call me Deacon Blues.* Some America. *I been through the desert on a horse with no name.* It was 1979. I kept going and going and going. I'd never walked so far all alone before. I came from a family where you had to be accompanied if you were so much as going to the corner store—and that was pretty unusual back in the day. I was astonished when I got to the highway. All those lights. All that noise. I was crossing the bridge over the Guadalupe, close to the Schreiner campus. It was a dream, but as clear as though I had conjured it, a night in my own real life. Someone tried to pick me up. I don't know if they were ready to kidnap me or take me back to my parents' house. I waved them away and they left me alone. I think it was around that time that I got to the park. I'd left my shoes. I think that's very important, having left my shoes. That's a detail here worth remembering. I was barefoot the whole way. I'd avoided cutting my bare feet. Nothing hurt. I remember how I wept. I wept as I did when I was thirty years old and newly divorced. As though I might kill myself and eliminate the world as I knew it, along with me. You can't imagine what that must've been, to be nine or ten years old and sobbing as though replete with two bottles of wine and half a bottle of Jose Cuervo. Suicidal. Who's suicidal at nine? It was surreal. And that's putting it lightly."

Paul paused.

"It was about that time that I approached the park, the same park I went to for Little League and running around and sneaking out for a covert joint with a girlfriend when I was in high school. I didn't recognize any of that, of course. I was nine when I tried out for Little League. I was fourteen when I snuck out with my first girlfriend. I recognized none of the trappings. Only the opening in the chain-link fence. There was the orangutan, orange and large and wise. I could pass through that hole and come out somewhere else entirely. I could be redeemed, I could bypass this nonsense of the world and everything in it, all its requirements and its prizes. Me in my Scooby Do PJs. I'd left my shoes. That was the important detail."

He wept then, as he had in a nine-year-old's dream, as he had at thirty in real life, drunk both times, unbelieving that this level of misery was possible in one person, unforgiving of the almighty who had appeared to him in the form of a great, orange orangutan that could just as easily have been conjured from an issue of *National Geographic*.

"I'm not sure how much stock one should take from dreams," he said at last. "But I tell you. I woke up that next morning feeling as though I had a choice. I could have followed that hairy old ape, into the woods, into the brush of that park. Who knows. I recall the distinct feeling that, had I said yes, you and I would not be together at this time, having this conversation."

The GP put his head in his hands. He did not want to answer the questions to come, though he knew he was bound to it.

For how long had he known Joel McKnight?

The good doctor: "Since our freshman year of college, I think. That makes over three decades. I was best man at both his weddings. He was best man at both mine, to Lisa, then to Ronnie."

For how long had he known Donna Avery-McKnight?

The good doctor: "I believe I was the one who introduced them. So. Twenty, twenty-five years? I'm having trouble managing time. I don't know if I'm missing a decade or if I'm erroneously adding one."

Was there ever any indication that they would do what they did?

The good doctor, steadfast: "Never." Then, weaker. "Because they didn't do it. The boy is missing. Again."

Had Paul the GP seen Allred before his second disappearance?

Paul the GP: "I'd heard what happened after it happened. That he'd changed. He'd transformed. He'd achieved that thing we all want, to be a kid again. But I don't think we realize the whole battle of living day-to-day when we're really, truly, actually kids. Imagine being that small again, knowing what you didn't know then. You must feel as though everyone bigger than you is just this side of taking a bite out of you. And for no other reason than because they can. You believe in a hierarchy when you're really, actually, truly that small. You like to think that there is a clockwork of cause and effect at hand, if x happens, then z will follow. You think there are rules. You think there are rules because the people above you, the Big People, perpetuate the idea. The thing is, the transition going from a real, actual, true kid to a Big Person is so gradual that you still abide by the idea that there are rules, though you can clearly see that there aren't. And it must go both ways. When you're observing the reverse, someone going back to a child, you must recognize that the rules you've set never meant anything to begin with. Because you never really abided by them to begin with. I think that's scarier, actually."

Paul the GP told another story. He'd watched a series of videos on YouTube, five minute features released by a combination wildlife resort and research facility in (he couldn't recall where) California or Arizona. The facility primarily serviced chimpanzees and their rehabilitation. There were six of them, three males, three females, each named for the vanara of the Indian epic, the *Ramayana*. The chimps feasted on organically grown, seasonally grown fruits and spoon-fed one another vegan meals of brown rice and beans, salads, chilis with tofu and without spice. They swung from old trees and frolicked in the river that was man-made and man-maintained. They dipped their feet and palms into non-toxic paint to make cards in thanks to their donors on Halloween and Thanksgiving and Christmas and Valentine's Day. They laughed hoarsely, off-key, like deaf people. They did not strike the viewer as capable of tearing off anyone's face. You might say that they were like very hairy toddlers, with albeit wiry limbs. Paul hesitated to call their humans captors, for the chimps' every whim, it seemed, was catered to. He said, "I wonder if they, the chimps, I wonder if they think that we think they're gods. Were I any of them, I wouldn't want to shatter the illusion. If someone wants to call me a god, I'd let them." He added that he had read a piece somewhere about great apes and their way of life, that in the wild, a troop of chimps or bonobos or orangutans are unlikely to migrate if their current situation satisfies their basic needs. A plentiful supply of food, clean water, shade, no predators in sight could result in a troop remaining where they were for decades.

Paul said, "But. We're not chimps. We're evolved, right? You would think that would mean certain things would've been ironed out. We'd know why we do what we do. And unlike the apes, knowing why we do what we do requires professional help. Or scripture."

He sighed, sipped from the can of peach-flavored sparkling water. He said, "So, let me rethink my answer. When you ask me if I thought that these two sane, stable, educated people would be capable of turning on their own child, my knee-jerk response is No. But my gut—my animal response—is that it's a free-for-all. You don't know what will make a good brain snap in two." He paused. "No, nix that. I think I do. It's envy. I mean, wouldn't you envy someone who has been given childhood for a second go-around? It's like redemption. You might grow up very, very differently."

When the children came together in their sacred bowery to discuss whether or not it would be a good idea to return home, three of them said outright that they would rather die. They were Clare, Evander, Mary Kathleen. They had not used those names in years. They had not wanted to because those names, in their old lives, had been a manacle. In this new life, they lived in one season, which was summer, which enabled them to go without clothes. And, if they stuck with those two laws handed down, in addition to those that they had established for themselves—and if the six of them stuck together, they could continue this way of life. They could continue to dream and exist day to day on fruit and a god who descended in slumber, in the form of an orangutan.

None of them had ever seen an orangutan in real life, not even in a zoo.

They did not want to see an orangutan in a zoo.

They did not want to go to college.

They did not want to become doctors or dancers or actors or construction workers or police officers or tinkers, tailors, soldiers, or sailors, for they know that to contribute to the pattern that they knew was to perpetuate more of the same resentment, the same greed and foulness. They would compare themselves to Taylor Swift and live to hate the lives they had before them.

And so, three of their number, when met with the suggestion to see how their folks were, chose to depart this world, perfect though they had made it. Clare, Evander, Mary Kathleen, found girthy vines from the fertile trees and hung from them, feet brushing the fringy grass. Billie Holliday sang of strange fruit, and it was what the surviving half of them imagined upon their discovery, like pomegranates in a pagan sacrifice.

Apes do not know what it is to self-destruct. They do not have that impulse, unlike their evolved relatives. It was a cruel maneuver of progress, the surviving three knew, that there was the possibility to exit at any time. It was something they had hoped to avoid, living as they did.

Before they decided to return to their families, they meditated on their intention. They did not know what they would do when they returned home. They did not know from where the impulse came, for they told themselves for as long as they had that this was home. They had been called to live in the woods. They had not any shape or form of a conceivable plan, for, what would they do when they got there. Go back to school, to repeat from the fourth grade on? To imitate the Big People? To believe in the notion of rules and cause and effect, when their own rules had functioned well enough for the six of them in the wilderness?

Clare, Evander, and Mary Kathleen indicated through gesture and gruff vocalizations (because they had long ago agreed not to speak) that to leave was to indicate that their way of life had been a failure, that their call to this place in the woods had been no more than a fantasy, as was the existence of God.

And so, the surviving members of their party woke on a sun dappled morning (as all other mornings had been for them in this area of divine providence, wherein everything, even clean water, was provided to them, free of charge) to find three of them hanging from thick vines from the thicker branches of a pomegranate tree.

The message: We would rather die than go back to the old life. Never mind our parents, our siblings. Never mind the note of change, whether or not the old landmarks of our childhood would still be there, the Burger King, the tennis courts, the old school. To change was to spoil, then rot outright.

Clare had been educated parochially, at St. Osanna of Mantua, in pleated, plaid skirts three inches below the knee, by kind and good nuns of that small order.

Evander had gone to the public school, where he had been dubbed gifted in letters but damned in numbers. His parents worried what his college scores might be, since he was in fourth grade and could barely add and subtract.

Mary Kathleen had been publicly educated, too, a

talent in song and dance, a future on Broadway, or so the people around her liked to think. She could do the hand-to-knee slap pattern that Bob Fosse devised for his rendition of "Dancin' Man", all in one go, where very few could. She was very adept. She was a gifted mimic. As the man sang, *Gonna leave my footsteps on the sands of time/If I never leave a dime.* And if that were all, she might have been happy enough. Though, in this world of ordinary and extraordinary folk, it would never have been enough.

God have mercy on us.

If you are there.

If we have dreamed of you.

Mrs. Livingstone prepared for the barbecue and for her elder daughters' arrival, singing, "*Bongo-bongo-bongo, I don't wanna leave the Congo, oh-no-no-no-no—*", a perfect mimic of Elaine Stritch on the stereo. She paused, remembering that her elder daughters were, in fact, her younger, that they had been in diapers when they'd last seen Julian, who was, in fact, their elder. They'd been in diapers or they'd been in kindergarten, too stupid to know anything either way, and they were completely enamored with their big sister.

It was all very confusing.

It was difficult to operate on any premise of normal.

Their big sister had, overnight, become smaller

than they were now. Julian, who had come home a naked, pagan, half-animal, who had metamorphosed to the nine-year-old who lived free or charge in the formative coils that made their near-thirty-year-old minds tick to this day, had never had a job, nor had she ever been educated beyond grade school. Her sisters, meanwhile, managed to make it through without her magic or her manipulations. They had graduated with honors from high school and college. They went into the law in some capacity, working for different firms as paralegals or underlings for paralegals. They paid their bills. They had circles of friends whom they joined for margaritas and trivia nights and movies. They dated. They seemed happy enough. And that's all you can hope for, isn't it? That's the best you can do.

Julian had always been seducing them, in one way or another. That was the problem: she always had some angle, some notion, and read something or heard somewhere that there was a way to maneuver around the rules. To her, the world had portals and incantations and unseen things. She read too many Roald Dahl type books, maybe that was it, wherein the kids are pitted against foully, hugely, grotesquely psychotic adults. Her third grade teacher assigned the class *James and the Giant Peach* for her last unit in reading. Mrs. Livingstone had thought, following her daughter's disappearance, that she ought to sue the school for every penny they had and run the name of that teacher (Mrs. Wight? Mrs. Blight?) through the mud.

You'll never teach third grade in this town again, Mrs. Whatever-your-name-is.

Twenty years later and coping with more metamorphoses and revelations than she could cope with, Mrs. Livingstone sliced red onion for hamburgers, assembled the makings of a big salad. She'd gone shopping, leaving Julian behind, knowing that her husband would lock her up in the dog's cage —and when she returned with her mountain of HEB bags, saw that she was right, for there her eldest was, peering out from between the thin black bars. She could probably have gotten herself out, Mrs. Livingstone thought, with a little finagling, or could have simply thrown a big enough tantrum that the cage would fall apart around her. But Julian hadn't. She was patient. She indicated that she wanted some of the raw ground-round for the burgers. At first, her mother said no. Julian, in her way, insisted, motioning that she was hungry.

She was wearing the clothes they'd kept when she left the first time, pink basketball shorts and a t-shirt commemorating the bats at Carlsbad Caverns. Her father unearthed the box in the cellar marked JULIAN and came upon a motherlode of shorts and overalls from Gap Kids and piles of t-shirts they'd picked up at Six Flags, the Alamo, Sea World, Universal Studios, the Pioneer Museum at

Fredericksburg, and told her to put them on or he would surely kill her, for it was within his rights to do so.

That was when times were simple, when they'd thought she'd been lifted from her room by an intruder. They took comfort in Elizabeth Smart, who had survived. They took even more comfort in JonBenét Ramsey, who had not. A predator was ordinary. It made sense.

What did not make sense (at least, at the time) was Julian's reason to leave, all on her own. It was confounding. It was insulting.

If there was a god, why would it choose their wicked, wicked child to join it in the place where heaven dipped down to touch planet earth—which happened to be in a city park, from the way their eldest told it? Why you and not me? Was that what all this boiled down to, the fact that there is a god and that you, after all, went unfavored? Julian had hated going to church, so much so that, one Saturday night when she was supposed to lay out a dress and tights and shoes for services the next day, she took a pair of scissors and made ribbons of every dress and every pair of tights and somehow jammed the conjoined blades through the soles of every good pair of Payless shoes, saying when her mother looked into her closet that she had nothing to wear.

Her mother declared (flippantly, of course) that her daughter was possessed and beyond hope and the family went to church without her. David Livingstone had worried then about leaving their nine-year-old at home alone, to which Mrs. Livingstone had replied, "Well, maybe we'll get lucky and she'll have run away by the time we get back."

No idle word is left unturned, so the Good Book says.

Did the Good Book have anything to say about runaways that slide back on the evolutionary scale, slide forward again and return for no other purpose than to affirm your notion that something beyond our ken is at hand, whose works do not feel like a test of faith, but a test of your sanity, a bully's teasing before the put-upon Poindexter snaps and shoots up his school? Her daughter in ape form had the look of a street person, reeking of body and greenery, her hair as overgrown and as matted as hanging moss. A street person was the worst fate that Mrs. Livingstone, or anyone else she knew, could think of. It meant that you did not fit, and if it meant that you did not fit, it meant that the people from whom you were descended did not, in some subtler way, did not fit either. It made Mrs. Livingstone feel exposed. Her daughter was not unwashed in the way of a hippie, for hippies, eventually, always cleaned up; Mrs. Livingstone had lived on a commune when she went by her own name, long before she earned her title of Mrs. She'd washed once a week and did not wear underwear for the duration of her stay there, and not a hair on her head was cut for one solid year. Still, she came to a breaking point, at which she decided that she could not abide one more day without running water, got her act together, and married a doctor who'd been honorably discharged from the army.

Jesus Christ, how can you live without a toilet? How do you shit where you stand? Why would you want to go back to that?

Elaine Stritch sang, "*Bongo-bongo-bongo, I don't wanna leave the Congo, oh-no-no-no-no*".

Mrs. Livingstone obliged her daughter in the dog house and fed her a bit of ground round from her hand. She shut off Elaine Stritch and put on Earth, Wind, and Fire, invoking better days, no children, no husband, the dirt and near-nakedness of the commune washing over her like the first high of some good, godly substance that she would only have once in a blue moon because it was so rare. It enabled her to multitask. She unpacked the rest of the groceries and put together the ingredients of a three-bean-bake, the raw bacon safely out of Julian's reach. She preheated the oven.

It enabled her, too, to ask her daughter what it was like out there in the woods.

She had seen her change from a creature she just barely recognized as a street person to a creature whose own habits she recalled in herself at that age: eating ground, raw meat, despite knowing how sick you could get; eating your own scabs; defecating in the bushes when a toilet was too far away. She was astonished to find how much she missed it, that wildness, that mess. It was, in fact, a holy experience, to be had once and taken away. You could not play Adam and Eve forever—that was something Julian's grandmother, her own mother, used to say, when the sight of her heathen daughter and pagan son coming in from the ravine with ringworm and rashes and benign pox and painted all over in runes made with crushed berries or their own blood, frankly, disgusted her. These were moments in which Mom threatened to lock them out, since they liked playing Adam and Eve so much. There was some implication of an incestuous ritual at hand between Mrs. Livingstone's brother and herself, completely false, but enough to place a soft barrier between the two of them that had grown more and more rigid as the years went by, giving them pause, making them wonder, making them sick and ashamed of something they hadn't done.

Julian said of the woods, "I liked it there."

No one had hurt her, and she had not felt the urge to hurt. The last was spoken with emphasis, having been freed of the urge to hurt. She told her mother the laws set down by their Maker, who had appeared to her in a dream as a great ape.

"What kind of ape?" Mrs. Livingstone asked, casual. She wanted to laugh: God was a great ape, why not?

"Big," Julian said. Her language was economical, not saying more than she needed. "Orange. Lots of stringy fur."

"An orangutan?"

Mrs. Livingstone lowered the temperature on the stove and went to find her phone. She found a video on YouTube of a female orangutan piloting a golf cart around the complex of a zoo in Florida. Whoever had uploaded the video added the *Sopranos* theme and the comments section was filled with references. Mrs. Livingstone hadn't seen much of *The Sopranos*, and so jokes about varsity athletes were lost on her. She went to Google and found a real photo, one taken of a male orangutan on a preserve in Borneo. He had small, intelligent eyes and the patient, open countenance of one who is in the midst of being interviewed between photo shoots, about his newly-published memoirs. Mrs. Livingstone imagined *The New York Times*, *The New Yorker*, unanimous praise. It would have a title like *My Life in the Woods*. No, that was stupid. *My Life of Bounty in Borneo*. He looked at the camera, then back to the interviewer, saying in an Ivy League tone, "—yes, my life in Borneo was, in a word, ah, bountiful."

She knelt in front of the dog cage to show Julian. Jules the dog, meanwhile, stepped daintily around the kitchen, huffing around for scraps.

Julian nodded. She told her mother what those two laws were: Thou shalt not kill and Do no harm. The rest were rules, man-made.

To Mrs. Livingstone, now that she had to really think about it, now that she was looking at her daughter through the bars of a dog cage while the dog itself roamed freely, the two laws that ought to be simple enough to follow were, in fact, two of those things that were easier said than done.

Thou shalt not kill.

Do no harm.

Mrs. Livingstone asked her daughter if they ate meat in the woods, or if it was a vegan diet. She told her a little about the commune, about making chocolate mousse with mashed avocado and macaroni and cheese with butternut squash and expired nutritional yeast.

To her question, Julian said, "Yes."

"Did you hunt boar or something? Rabbits?"

"No."

"What did you hunt?"

"Nothing."

"How did you get any meat if you didn't hunt?"

Julian told her, very plainly, what had become of their party in the woods. The three who would rather have died than come back had done just that, as was within their rights, their choice. The surviving members mourned in their way. They held a vigil around the tree from which the bodies of Clare, Mary Kathleen, and Evander swung. They prayed for three days until a collective dream from God as the great orangutan told them to eat of this fruit and bury their dead.

Mrs. Livingstone thought of that Billie Holliday song, "Strange Fruit". But in the song, it was someone else who had made humans into dripping, swinging vegetation. It had not been voluntary. She shuddered, for it was a hideous end, for a criminal as for an innocent. Though she herself had considered a premature exit (in her own bed, she'd featured, all the pills in the house plus as many cocktails as she wanted, with something like *Roseanne* or *Seinfeld* on the TV), she always managed to step back from the edge. It repelled her as much as murder.

Thou shalt not kill.

Do no harm.

She asked her daughter why she came back at all.

Julian said, "To see if anything was different."

"Is it?" Mother asked.

"It's worse," Daughter replied.

Mother had been about to ask, in what way. But she nixed that. She nodded, for she knew that it was, in many creeping ways, worse. The computer made it worse. She's said so from the day the dial-up men came to install the internet in their home for the first time. Since that day, she came to refer to all invisibly connected things, from Facebook to Bluetooth, collectively, as the computer. Never mind the fact that she herself and everyone she knew was on Facebook, and posted every stupid triumph as though they were all, in some minor way, celebrities with fan bases who were owed every stupid triumph. Never mind that the fan bases were waiting, just as eagerly, for your failures. They drooled over failures, your misquote, your poor choice of words, your misfired joke, your losing your cool in an argument over nothing with someone who was a friend of a friend. You didn't have to worry about that in the days before the computer. People used to shrug and forget about it. Now, they seemed happy to brand you a racist or a sexist or an anti-Christian or a demon because enough people had seen what you said and took sides and would not let anyone forget. What killed Mrs. Livingstone was the sanctimony. Because everyone she knew in the days before the computer had been racists and sexists and anti-Christians and demons. Now, on the computer, everyone behaved as though they had never even dropped an F-bomb.

But, as the Good Book said, "No idle word will be left unturned."

Or something like that.

Julian nodded, then shook her head. She left before there was any Facebook. She came back and now there were more places to expose yourself than you could shake a stick at. The concept must be positively alien to her. She was too young to be on Facebook back then.

She listened to her mother and said, bluntly, "I want to go home."

But Julian couldn't go home. Not now, not while

the guests were just pulling up in their respective Toyotas with their father waving in the driveway as though everything were just so. Through the window, he motioned quickly, frantically, for his wife to let the creature out of her cage.

Mrs. Livingstone did so, and Julian emerged, the picture of what she had been at nine years old. She had shrunken to that height and her ape hair had fallen out. Her feet had realigned to look like feet. Her hair was long and combed, and she stood still long enough for her mother to pull it back into a scrunchie. To her younger sisters, who had grown up and lived and worked and made profiles on Facebook, among other places, it would be as though Julian had never budged an inch. Thank God they had never seen their sister in any other way. Thank God for the metamorphosis.

Mrs. Livingstone nudged her eldest toward the door to meet them properly, hands on her shoulders. The dog yipped to announce them.

When asked if she knew what her husband was about to do, Mrs. Livingstone put her head in her hands and said, "I was shot, too, you know. I kicked the door open for her. I told her to get her ass in gear and run for it while she could. It's what any mother would do, with any sense of decency."

Marisol Enamorado said of her situation, "I'd decided I'd had enough. Just like that. I'd decided I'd had enough, and that was enough."

She was not an angel of death, as wives who annihilate their children are said to be. She did not add arsenic to anyone's oatmeal. She used what was immediate and available. She used one of the paring knives with a porcelain blade, one that she never let anyone touch because the material was delicate and chipped easily, not dishwasher safe, expensive, part of a set.

"I didn't think I could do it," she said of it later, "I didn't think I had it in me. I think that was what made me go after him."

It was bright, just after three in the afternoon. It was when you think you'd reached the point at which the day's activity had tapered off, nothing could alter the humdrum and all would remain this way until tomorrow. It is such a blessing, after all, to have a dull day. This was a silent transformation, as when one hour becomes another, mid-afternoon to late afternoon. Though Marisol Enamorado could not have said what the difference was, what had made her decide to take the knife and find her son, one minute wondering if she should use up the rest of the sweet potatoes for dinner, the next consummate, full-on infanticide, she did know that something had been switched, ON and OFF—or rather, OFF then ON, like some beastly instinct that indicated when she could bear no more of this nonsense.

When she could bear no more of this nonsense, as

though this were all an elaborate prank. She knew that God was not mocked. But what about when her Maker mocked her?

"I'd wanted to call this a lot of devil stuff," she said.

She'd wanted to call it a lot of devil stuff because it turned what she knew about order and progress on its head. Backward and then forward and then back again, right where you started. Nine was the perfect age at which to start anew.

Marisol Enamorado would never be nine years old again, she knew that. Nor would she ever know what God was, firsthand. She knew that, too.

She looked at her husband first, envying his forgetfulness. He did not quite know who she was these days, often mistaking her for his mother or one of his sisters, all of whom had adored him. It made sense to long for those for whom the word adoration could be applied. As far as Marisol knew, no one had ever adored her. Enjoyed, yes. Cared for, yes. Tolerated (a sneaking suspicion), more often than not. Adored, never. It must be unconditional. It must be without boundaries. It must be mutual, wherein neither party has to reach for it.

Alonso had reached for God, and God had reached for her son.

But not me. Never mind how often I've reached for you, you unfeeling, invisible stink. Permeating, creeping around, one minute there's nothing, the next it's a full-on assault, exactly like a fart. That's what you are.

So, she left her husband alone and went to look for her son.

"I found him in his room," Marisol said. "I think he thought he was safe in there."

Pam Jones

They Use Tools

"Two things happened," Donna Avery-McKnight said. "I ran into the boy's mother at the grocery store. What was his name? Evan? Evander, yes, Evander. I'd seen her only once, and that was the day the bench in the park was commemorated. It wasn't as though it'd been a big ceremony. I think it was just us, just the families. We couldn't have a funeral because whether or not our children were dead was up in the air. And the idea of them being alive somewhere was too horrible to think about. Maybe they'd been sold. Maybe the girls had been given in marriage to—" She swallowed, her mind fouled suddenly by this other notion of marriage. "I thought a lot about a movie I saw in college. *120 Days of Sodom*, adapted from the Marquis de Sade novel. I couldn't watch most of it at the time, I had my hands in front of my face. But I do recall feeling just a bit jealous of the fascists who took all the captives from that little village. Kind of a curiosity, like, what must that be to put all scruples to one side and just succumb to—" She did not want to finish, but found the gumption to continue. "—to your impulses. I was relieved that I wasn't the only one who fantasized about feeding someone a handful of my own waste."

Joel was silent.

Donna went on. "It wasn't sexual. But it was primitive. Apes kill their own young, don't they? Because they don't smell right. For something as small as that."

Joel, who was not the boy's father, did not look at his wife.

"I'd seen Evander's mother," Donna said, and repeated it as though each recitation of the opening line might tell a slightly more mitigating story. "She was in the salad dressing aisle. I was going this way, she was going the other. With our two carts facing one another, it looked like the face-off in a joust. She knew who I was and I knew who she was. This is not to say that we are both very distinct looking people. But you have all that data in your brain. And it arranges itself when the moment comes, when you see that face."

They continued to shop, not quite looking at the other, save from out of the corner of one eye, save for some pheromone that they each exuded and detected in the other, moving down the aisle to pick up ranch dressing, barbecue sauce, olives that neither of them needed.

"In a perfect world, we might have been a comfort to each other." Donna Avery-McKnight's voice was matter of fact and far away. "We might've been friends."

As it was, Allred McKnight's mother envied Evander's for her status. There was dignity in a child who predeceases you. There was shame in its opposite. Its opposite was living, yes, but mutable. A changeling was at once private and writ large. Donna Avery-McKnight had not brought her son shopping with her since he became small again. It would, of course, confuse the people who had already seen him, the checkout gals, the guys at the sushi bar, the manager who oversaw the ten-items-or-less line who was always so patient and who was called something like Shari or Sharon. Donna couldn't very well re-introduce her son as her grandson because, first of all, it would be a lie, and secondly, because Allred had not let her touch a hair on his head since they had seen the old-old house, much less get in a car with her or Joel.

What was worse?

What was worse? A child who had been kidnapped? Or a child who had died, horribly, assaulted, used up and left for scraps, which amounted to the same thing as a child who had been kidnapped because some part of them would always be missing? Or was it more humiliating to have one of those kids who wandered home after having left to "find themselves"? There were a number of them these days, that breed of offspring that was more and more the norm, who somehow could not hack the unspoken expectation that, despite economic downturns and upsets of brain electricity, you were on your own, that your troubles, plus those of the big, wide world were no longer the responsibility of anyone but you, God help you and save you. This breed of offspring went off to college or eloped with the love of their life, only to come crawling back, following a breakdown, a break-up, a development of a drinking habit, a gambling problem, doctor shopping, excommunication from a cult. These creatures hid themselves away in their old bedrooms, behind the American Girl collection, the Lego fortresses, and wrapped themselves up in their flannel sheets, still smelling faintly of all the accidents they'd had at two in the morning between toddlerhood and age (embarrassingly) twelve-and-a-half.

Donna Avery-McKnight recalled a *Cosby* episode in which the eldest Huxtables met some strife and, for one reason or another, made the tentative sojourn home. Wherein, Dr. Heathcliff Huxtable, lovable and fair, stomped around the cozy brownstone, declaring, "They are not going to live HERE."

She would rather her son had died.

The second thing that happened was when she turned the corner, and who should be there in the line for the pharmacy but—"—that girl's mother. Not Mary Kathleen, the other one. Clarissa. Clare? That's it. She didn't see me, but I saw her."

Donna Avery McKnight abandoned her cart to stand directly behind her. She undulated her head on its stalk, her neck taut, like someone possessed. She considered biting her ear, whether she might gnaw a piece out of the cartilage or take the whole thing off, she had not decided, and did not have to when she felt a hot breath on the back of her own neck not unlike the hot breath she surely dispensed on the back of Mrs. Clare's-Mother's neck. She, like Mrs. Clare's-Mother, did not turn around. Donna Avery-McKnight did not turn around because if she did, she knew that Evander's mother would surely have made a decision, whether it was to take a bite out of Allred's mother's face or her beating heart was up to her. What they must have looked like. What they must have looked like if anyone knew who they were and what they were about: like a worm of three segments, each quivering on the brink of ravenous self-destruction, the head bending backward to eat the end first.

My God, my God.

But God had not answered Donna Avery-McKnight. He or She or It had answered her son, who would not look at her.

"I could not stand it any longer," she said.

She stepped from the pharmacy line. The mothers of the dead children (for disappeared equaled dead) let her go and stood stark still for a moment before letting someone else, a little old man come to get his diabetes medication, fill the gap between them.

Her son, when last seen, was in the garden. He'd been sitting out there for an hour before she left, unresponsive to her when she told him that she was going to the store and just as stony when she asked if there was anything special he'd like. He still had the CD player, the mixed CD that Joel gave him, playing and replaying the same song, Todd Rundgren's "Change Myself". The earbuds had been replaced by headphones that pillowed his ears and shut out everything else, save for Todd Rundgren. *How can I change the world/When I can't change myself?*

Donna said, "He couldn't hear me, so it was easy enough to step behind him."

When asked if that was when she put her hands around the boy's throat and squeezed, Joel nodded.

When asked why he failed to stop her, for he, too, was there in the garden, picking ripe jalapeños from the potted plants, he could only say that he was rooted to the spot by an involuntary, primitive notion that to move was to indicate his presence. "And then she would've come after me, probably."

But the boy freed himself.

Joel said, "He did."

And when the boy freed himself, had Joel's wife come after him, as was his assumption?

Joel said, "No, she did not. It was as though she'd

come out of a fugue. She asked what had happened. We asked each other what had happened to Al."

Joel had seen it.

"Yes," Joel said. "I mean, we asked where Al had gone. Because he was gone."

Again.

Marisol Enamorado caught her son around the waist and pinned him to her from behind. They sank to the floor. The room was ringed with artifacts from the old life—as she had begun to define the years, as divided into thirds which were Alonso's pre-disappearance, the middling decades wherein she waited for the other shoe to drop, and these wild weeks following his return. She had seen him as a man, which was to say she saw him as an animal, and had to reconcile his furred and filthy presence among her boy's things. Now that he was a boy again, she could not trust him for fear that he might change into something else, something that was overtly Hadean that would confirm a mother's worst suspicions, about her son and herself.

There was the plastic tub of loose Lego bricks. There were old cases of chipped colored pencils and dried, spongy markers and the doodles produced with them, commemorations of heroic acts from cartoons or tales from the Old Testament. There were figurines and fantasy scenes frozen in time. There was his first Bible, annotated, with illustrations in puffy pastels.

There was his grown-up Bible, received for his ninth birthday, with his name stamped on the cover in gold. There were his chapter books: complete series of *Redwall*, *Horrible Histories*, Roald Dahl and C.S. Lewis and Jean Craighead George. There were his picture books: *The Salamander Room*, the *Arthur* books, the *Frog & Toad* books, a book that made her tear up every time she looked at it called *Love You Forever*. All of them slightly soiled with pages thumbed, covers frayed in the corners, one thousand occasions in which he begged her to read them again and again and again.

She inserted her fore and middle fingers into both nostrils so as to pull his head back, expose his throat. She put the porcelain blade to the pulsing point just under his left ear.

"I'd never killed anything in my life," she said, her voice gauzy. "I suppose that's still true. He's gone, not dead. He made a noise." A whimper, a sob, something that would draw upon her sympathies. He was cunning, as animals and children and street people are wont to be. "He bit me. Look." Marisol pushed her sleeve to her elbow to show a ring pitted into her forearm into which small teeth had sunk. He'd broken the skin. She'd bled and he did, too, for the blade had made a small but deep incision under his ear, and the carpet was spotted when she came to and discovered that she was alone in Alonso's bedroom.

To commemorate the family reunion, the grill was hot. There was a three-bean bake in the oven and a fringy salad overflowing the bowl and two kinds of potato chips, plain and jalapeño ranch. A choice of Sprite, root beer, or Coke. A platter of brownies from the bakery at HEB and the patio glowing pink from the festoonery, chili lights unearthed from the boxes of Christmas decorations in the attic. The stereo played a soundtrack that invoked simpler if not better times, that which would inspire a sense of order in the three Livingstone girls, so that they might remember who the bosses were. It was Mrs. Livingstone's choice, as disc jockey, Chris Rea's *On the Beach*, Carly Simon's *Greatest Hits* live at Martha's Vineyard.

Teresa and Susanna were as enamored with their older sister as they had been in childhood, though they were grown and Julian, as far as they knew, remained an unchanged, picture-perfect image of the girl who lived in their memories and their dreams. They were around thirty and Julian was still nine, and they practically knelt before her. They, in their high-heeled shoes, who had driven themselves in reliable Toyotas, who knew how to dress for success, plus do their own hair and makeup.

Their older sister had her hair long and ponytailed, in Gap overalls and a t-shirt that had been tie-dyed green and blue at a Y camp activity. Teresa and Susanna still thought, in the backs of their minds, of day camp at the local YMCA to be a very grown up, big kid thing, as they did with gifted programs and advanced reading groups and Shark level swimming, though by now they were college graduates and had lost their respective virginities. Teresa went to AA and Susanna smoked enough weed to put herself in a permanent cloud. They hated adulthood. They were resentful that the elder generation did not know what they were doing either. They'd missed their sister terribly and had not been let to invoke her name too often, lest her disappearance suggest something unsavory—perhaps what it had been all along, the suspicion that Julian had left of her own free will.

Their mother wanted to tell them that they should have been there to see Julian as an ape. Julian furred with feet like hands. No tail, but her canine teeth were long and pointed. Mrs. Livingstone had shuddered when her eldest smiled, for she knew that apes did not grin unless they were threatened.

Now.

Now, when she smiled her teeth were round and small and falling out. One canine tooth and one upper incisor made a hole that caused Julian to suck her upper lip, issuing idiotic, slurping sounds, giving her the look of a hillbilly. She had shoes on her feet, white Keds that her mother bought for the occasion. She'd allowed her mother to comb and weave her long hair into a French braid. Her overalls did not bunch to accommodate the diaper she still had to wear, though it seemed that since her metamorphosis, she'd remembered how to use a toilet—when her mother let her out of the dog cage, Julian had run for the bathroom while Mrs. Livingstone waited, pacing, in the hall, and silently celebrated the ordinary noise of flushing, splashing, the ordinary nagging when the girl emerged to wipe down the mirror when she was through washing her hands. As a reward, Julian was allowed to feed the dog and change her water.

Good girls.

Good dogs.

"I don't know where my husband was," Mrs. Livingstone said.

"I thought we might go into the backyard," Mrs. Livingstone said.

She started the grill herself and the girls, led by Julian, followed.

It might have been at this point that Teresa and Susanna, possessed by some primeval instinct and motivated by the most holy idea that something of childhood (its guilessness, its rudeness, its inability to tell time) could be regained, took off their high-heeled shoes.

Mrs. Livingstone said, "I hadn't noticed. Or, rather, I had noticed, but I didn't think anything of it. High heels are hell. I wasn't going to tell them off. If I'd thought that was all they were going to do. If I'd known what else that they were going to get up to, I wouldn't have left. If I'd known what my husband was going to do. If I'd known what was going to happen—"

She laughed, winced, her injured shoulder.

"That old saying leaps to mind. If wishes were fishes, we'd have some to fry, wouldn't we?"

Alonso knew where Aleah lived from memory and from Facebook. He tore through backyards, through azaleas and raspberry canes and rosemary, until he recognized the backyard that she still occupied, as the world had since grown more expensive and Aleah had yet to move out.

His hair had been cut. His clothes were torn from the struggle through thorn and bramble; they, like Julian's were preserved as relics and brought out when the grown-up things swamped him. Cargo shorts and a Hawaiian shirt, tiny Teva sandals with Velcro straps, smelling of mothballs and the basement. His teeth were missing and his ear had been cut, for he knew he left a trail from what he still thought of in his mind as the old home (as opposed to the only one, the real one, visualized in a dream, realized, and which was fading now from his mind as a whole lifespan in the fog of dementia), three and a quarter miles. He wondered if she would recognize him now. He wondered if she would love him.

His father did not quite recognize him.

He wondered if that was what set his mother off.

Aleah's yard was small but trim, dominated by one large live oak with branches that cast a wide, green canopy from fence to fence. Her parents, he remembered, scattered bluebonnet seeds into the grass which would come up in violet patches in the spring. It was summer now, and the grass prickled underfoot like splinters when Alonso removed his sandals. These, he threw with babyish, comical muscle, one with a bang into a plastic wading pool, the other upsetting a stone birdbath. The pool, he remembered, was for bathing their dogs, and a wave of gritty water slopped over the edge when the sandal hit. He hooted, listened, waited, and a trollish-looking creature came huffing and sneezing to the sliding glass door, a pug or a bulldog mix with rolling marble eyes and a brindle pattern in its fur. It was not fierce; it was too phlegmy. Its noises were those of a friendly household moron, as opposed to any kind of sentinel, announcing guests and intruders with equal excitement. Its glee was such that it urinated where it stood on its side of the glass. They observed each other with mutual interest.

An idea came to him, not unreasonable, that he could adapt to its ways and perhaps Aleah would take him in as a second pet. He could be the protector, taking up what the squash-faced dog lacked. They could entertain their mistress, chasing tennis balls and gutting plush rabbits for the squeaking mechanism inside, growling at the UPS people and Amazon trucks and passersby. It could be done.

The door slid on its track, and Alonso ducked behind the tree trunk, and the troll that was called

Roo or Boo strutted out into the yard, coaxed by a woman's voice coming from behind the glass. The dog found him at once. Alonso knelt, allowed the animal to sniff him all over, his crown, the spirals of his ears, his neck his underarms that no longer bore that astonishing odor of having been a man, which is also to have been a creature. Now, a boy again, he no longer stunk. He no longer had to police himself as he found he'd had to do, the older he got. He sniffed and that was enough to break the levy in him, which the dog was happy enough to lap up for the salt, the stickiness. As a man, though the rules were clear, he might nevertheless have been tempted. Even in the woods. Even in the woods, though fruit was plentiful and he'd wanted for nothing, he might have wanted meat. He might have thought, more than once, of taking a rock to the dog's head, for it was small and domesticated and would not know any better. It had been easier as a boy.

It had been easier as a boy because he, too, had been small, if not domesticated.

He was glad for this second transformation, the relief of a grown man's burdens.

Roo or Boo knew that he was a comfort and made quick work of cleansing and grooming this, a fellow beast. Alonso pulled the Hawaiian shirt over his head (working the buttons escaped him) and dipped it into the gritty water from the wading pool, dabbed at the wound under his ear. The palm trees and rolling surf pattern, the blue and green motif, was darkly stained and smelled of rust. The collar was damp, still, with mild gore. He would heal, it had not reached the vital throat. With the shirt's hem, he gave his face a thorough scrub. He let the dog touch his tongue to that place under the boy's ear.

In a minute, the gap closed, the tissue knitted.

In another minute, there was not a scar.

Alonso blessed the animal and decided to remain where he was. The woods seemed farther away, thus impossible to reach, unless through that queer access of a dream or a daydream or the call of the great ape that he, perhaps, had conjured himself.

Like his father, who did not quite remember his son, wherein one day he did, the next he did not.

Like Alonso's father, the son imitated a gesture and uttered a phrase that the boy had heard the man say, years ago, when something had either disgusted, confounded, or exasperated him. Alonso could not recall what those things might have been: Mayonnaise on a sandwich? The election process, because he did recall that his father did not vote and now could not? The early signaling of his own mind blurring, erasing words, names? The boy shook his head until he felt his ears wobble. And he said, affecting the same brief, gruff laugh, "No thanks, no thanks."

He did not know if he could go back to the woods. He might not know what to do anymore. They, if the miracle of anyone else's return were open to them, might not receive him.

But he was a boy again. Alonso said thanks for that and reaffirmed the plan to learn from Roo or Boo. He would start now. Arching his body, palms flat on the ground, he positioned himself as dogs do when they are ready to play. The dog, knowing what it meant, did the same and, in its kind, snuffling way, corrected the boy on his stance, to fix his legs lower to the ground so as not to appear too much bigger than his playmate, for this was not true aggression, and not to bare his teeth. The boy was a keen pupil. He was an enthusiastic one, to boot, for his howls and gnarrs were loud enough to provoke the mistress of the house, Aleah, to emerge.

She was not wearing the bronze-colored Sunday dress. On this day, a weekday, a Friday, she had on black, around-the-house leggings and a t-shirt, voluminous, beige, with sleeves that ended at her elbows. Her hair was loose and long. And, Alonso could see, she came into the yard with such haste that she'd forgotten to put on her shoes. He hid behind the tree, his small paw in his mouth and watched her crane her neck and call for the dog, to continue to crane even when Roo or Boo waddled to her and grunted around her ankles like a ham on legs.

She stood on the wooden deck. Her eyes narrowed at the big tree. She called, "Hello?" once, twice, again, stepping down, starting, hissing, hopping into the yard on one foot because, as Alonso noted, she'd picked up a splinter. She sat on the bottom step to examine the sole, angling that leg to balance that foot on her knee. Another observation by the boy: that the leggings were old and the fabric was worn thin in some places, and that the seams had broken in the groin of them, and that with her ankle perched in this way, he could see that because they were around-the-house clothes, she was not wearing underwear. A small exposure, a shock of dark hair.

That day in the river, when he'd been a man, she'd pulled him away from the drooling crowd, deep into the brush (not the woods), far off the trail. She'd pulled the bronze-colored dress over her head and showed him everything and left him panting and orgasming and astonished in the shade of a squat cedar until one of the men he recognized from church, a regular trail hiker, found him and covered him with a sweatshirt. Guiding Alonso with one hand on his elbow, the sweatshirt tied like a loincloth around his waist, the man from church asked him was he'd been doing out there. Aleah had told him not to say a word, and Alonso did not, and the people from church did not expect him to have a concrete grasp of language. He kept silent as the man brought him to the parking lot, loaded him into his car and drove him home.

Alonso remembered, then as now: Thou shalt not kill and Do no harm. He'd done neither. He pushed the other rules to one side. He'd been thinking of the lifting hem of that bronze dress ever since.

Roo or Boo announced the intruder, the guest, the boy, the creature who did not live here, but who might or might not belong here. It was up to him to reveal himself, and so he did. Aleah's head came up with her eyes flashing because she did not yet recognize who it was, only the shape of someone small who was alien to her. When her vision cleared, still hazy, she saw that it was only a boy, one who could be any number of boys in this neighborhood who cut through yards looking for lost balls or glider planes or Frisbees or boomerangs, who waited at any number of cul-de-sacs for the school bus to come in the fall, and who went chasing after dogs and sprinklers and ice cream trucks in the summer. When the rest of her senses electrified and put things together, memory and image, a wisp from the past that had traveled years to land right here, in this trim, tidy yard, she remembered (the river, the park, off the path, the shade of a squat cedar) and she beckoned.

Alonso, dropping to his knees, canine, submissive, playing, crept over. On all fours, he ducked his head shyly. She patted his crown, laughed when he licked it, just as she had when the dog emitted its sounds of devotion, huff and puffs that came with mucous from the back of its throat. Alonso echoed, a good mimic, and to his greatest joy, it made her laugh more.

She put up one finger, bade him to wait, and went

inside. Boy and dog waited and squinted into the shadowy kitchen from the bright backyard. When she came out again, she had with her a set of tweezers and a carton of grape tomatoes. Since his return, Alonso had not liked to eat the fruit bought at the grocery store; it was always underripe and never as flavorful as what he'd had in the woods. But he eyed them now as she took one from the carton in her fingers like a jewel and tossed it up into the air. It made a high, red arc and landed with a bounce in the grass. When the dog bounced away, Alonso followed its lead. There ensued a quick mock-struggle as the two teethed at it, gently, so as to keep it from bursting, and the boy allowed the dog the first victory. It trotted back with the tomato between its stubs, for how could you call them teeth, and dropped it at Aleah's foot that kept her anchored while she poked at the other on her ankle with the tweezers. She paused at her work to throw another tomato. This time, it struck the boy full in the chest and, because he was a good dog, he fell on his paws to take it in his mouth. Determined to keep his teeth from grazing it, he secured it in his puckered lips, his mouth small but full. A failed endeavor, for when a squirrel materialized on the bird feeder hanging from the tree, it was Roo's or Boo's prerogative to frighten it away with a more ferocious warning than it had issued toward the boy, and the tomato broke, oozing between his teeth.

Aleah was amused, more so, maybe, by Alonso's

quivering chin, the wavering fullness of his eyes. And so, when the dog returned to nuzzle at her ankle, Alonso, light with gratitude, did the same. He lapped at her instep. He fixed his paws on her thigh to taste her underfoot and found the splinter. He nipped at her toes when she cried out. Though he knew where everything was, and though he knew that he had experienced everything a man had to experience only weeks before, the mechanics of it escaped him. No, try it this way, more on the nose. The mechanics of it frightened him. The act of love had been a terrifying thrill, like a mouse taken up by a hawk, thrown in midair, caught, and thrown to its death before being consumed, bones and all. The act of love was not love itself. The idea struck him and froze him, a grown person's big toe in his mouth, the nail lacquered gold, and her hand was now a claw in his hair. And, out of a blue sky, the air changed. He understood their difference, his smallness, her womanhood over him, though if you were to place their birth certificates side by side, he was the elder by four years. But, as it was, he was a child and she was not. Her smell was hideous. Her eyes were venomous. To remember the shade of the squat cedar was to recollect a nightmare, and he knew right there and then that he did not want this.

When he was really and truly nine, a memory surfaced of something overheard, on TV or a conversation between grown-ups to which he shouldn't have been privy. What stood out to him was this: That humanity was at the top of the animal kingdom, but children were at the bottom of humanity's food chain.

Another recollection. Again, when he was really and truly nine, and when Aleah was really and truly five, he'd coaxed her into the cloakroom at church. There had been a promise of some token, a sleeve of M&Ms from the candy machine, if Aleah would let him do X, Y, and Z to her. There were rows and rows of trench coats and pea coats and sweaters and shawls. There were so many that the hangers did not rattle on the bar. She had panted and sniffed. She had not quite refused. She had wept. She had not the brains to know what was happening, and to be fair, at the time, neither had Alonso, save for the vile, glowing amusement that he had her, the smaller, where he wanted her, and the certainty that the two would emerge from the cloakroom and slide back into their Sunday school seats without any exchange of M&Ms at all.

He'd seen other boys do the same thing to other girls. He'd seen other girls do the same thing to other boys. He'd seen other girls do the same thing to other girls, and he'd seen other boys do the same thing to other boys. Even if no one knew exactly what it was they were doing.

It was what you did.

When he dropped her toe from his mouth, his

face was one of disgust. When Aleah registered his disgust, she did not hesitate to kick Alonso full in the face. The force of it sent him staggering backward, walking on his heels, kicking up dirt and grass. He descended and tasted blood in his mouth, having bitten his tongue. That was when Roo or Boo fancied the boy to be no less than an invasive squirrel; its nubby teeth were no less powerful within the mechanism of a quick working jaw that opened and closed on Alonso's ear, his cheek, his bare arms and shoulder, all of which the boy turned to offer the dog rather than allow it one taste of his blood.

In this neighborhood, children often shrieked. Usually, it was out of excitement, a hoot of triumph at being crowned King or Queen of the Castle or a feral emission that burst from the gut at the singular pleasure that came from just running around with no one to stop you. Other times, when it was not a joyful noise, it was one of frustration, a wail at being left out, of missing the ball a moment too late, of a firm and foul NO to the question of being allowed to do this or that. A scoff from someone bigger than you, a mocking condolence, "Poor baby." A stern admonishment to Get Over It and Walk It Off.

Alonso's happened to be one howl out of many in that moment, a chorus of victors and outcasts and mourners of lost Frisbees. He vibrated with his own sound, no bigger than any other, as it turned out, on this block. When Aleah came upon him and took his ankle, he was muffled only briefly by the dirt and a bit stupefied at why the fence was getting farther and farther away from him. Over his shoulder, Aleah's kitchen was dark and cool, neither one a luxury now, for he knew that if she brought him, dragging him as she was by one ankle, into her lair (for what else was it?) smelling of bananas and laundry with sounds of a *Cosby* rerun churning somewhere in its deeper intestine, he would never get out.

(Was it the episode where Rudy wanted to wear a summer dress to a birthday party on a cold afternoon, and Claire told her she couldn't?)

He'd nearly given up. He'd almost grown contented with the idea that Aleah might follow through with that most hideous, ultimate fate told of in fairy tales: That she might put him in a pot and eat him, alive or boiled. He did not want to imagine anything else, for it was all too complex for his mind, now that he was nine again.

His fingers grazed a thing in the grass that was foreign and sharp and cold. Had Aleah forgotten the tweezers entirely? Alonso himself had always feared tweezers, and he was amazed to find that he was holding a pair now, dropped, it seemed, by his captor in her rush to catch him. He associated the dreaded tweezers with ten thousand splinters, hating the necessary instrument more than any threat spun by his mother of potential infections, as a result avoiding the wooden deck at his own house, despite the fact that he went barefoot everywhere else in his life and picked up splinters just as easily.

In the woods, he remembered, you tried to be as gentle as you could when someone got a splinter. What he could not remember was how they got the splinters out.

Alonso wriggled and turned and lunged and pinched.

Neither had anyone heard Aleah on the block that day, and she would not tell anyone about the funny-looking cut she'd gotten on the back of her calf, as though the mandibles of a large insect had open and shut there. And, because she couldn't think of anything better, when her mother came home from the treadmills at the YMCA, Aleah would tell her that it was a bug bite.

As for Alonso, he was still before ducking back through the fence, through the loose plank that swung open to the sidewalk, because he wanted to know if it was too late, then and now, to apologize.

As for Allred Avery-McKnight, for all anyone, including himself knew, he did really and truly vanish from his parents' backyard, and rematerialized in the gauzy heat of the town park. By the bleed in the sky, it was hours later, and the bench on which he sat cast long shadows across the grass. His shape rippled as if motivated by its own agitation and the crown of its head touched the tall chain link fence around the tennis court directly across. He had the CD player with him, still going, a different song now, the one that came after Todd Rundgren, Grace Jones's "Slave to the Rhythm". He'd listened to Todd Rundgren so much that any deviation from the pattern was a shock to his system, and he tore the noise-canceling earphones from his head. The CD player went with it and struck the chain link fence, the case cracking, the battery compartment snapping open, the batteries bouncing into the tennis court.

He took in the environs. He took in the environs in a way that he hadn't since he left the woods. Like a cat using its vomeronasal organ, he dropped his mouth open to help his nose gather as many odors as he could, and to taste them.

Of the six children who had lived in the woods, he had been the most modest, the least likely to be rough when they engaged in wrestling games or took sides to play War. He thought that was where things changed. When they played War, they took sides. Usually, it became boys against girls. He hadn't liked that because he could not lead and the other boys wasted time arguing strategy, and he felt that the girl (the one who wound up leaving the woods with them) made the best captain, anyway, for she had been the competent one among them.

He had never known her name, as he had not known the names of the others. They had from the start agreed not to tell one another their names, with the hope that they would all one day forget them. The children's names became a secret they each held, privately, silent everywhere save for their own separate minds. A certain shame came with the recollection, at waking each morning and remembering what he had been called and the various associations that came with the name Allred. It had been his father's name, and he had not seen his father since he and his mother went to live with his grandmother. But that was not the shame of it; the shame of it was the attachment and the grasping of images and memories that did not belong to him, that he did not want. He reasoned that if you had a name, everyone knew it, and if everyone knew it, it meant that anyone could find you. You had to have a name in order to grow up.

His parents did not like to get the mail because it was all for them. Not letters or gifts, but bills and notices for jury duty and notes from passive aggressive neighbors who wrote to complain about a tree that Joel cut down that was technically on their side of the property line. As retaliation, Joel sheared down their azalea bush to a fringy stub because at least half of the blooms dripped over onto his side of the fence. There ensued a cold war between them and the people next door, first with notes, then with calls to the police about small or invented noise or trespasses or petty thefts. A look was soon read as harassment. They, his mother and stepfather, enunciated their offenders' names into the phone to the exhausted dispatcher. Allred could mimic the tone in his stepfather's voice, imperious, callous, one hand on his hip: "John and Judy Bouvier. Yes, Mister Jo-ohn and Missus Joo-dee Boo-vee-yay." He could imitate his mother, who loomed over Joel's shoulder during these calls, her mouth stretched and sour, arms tight and folded across her black turtleneck.

He had the idea that his mother and stepfather were going to kill John and Judy Bouvier, but they never did. This theory faded out when he came home and the Bouviers came over, having apparently made amends during his twenty-year absence, more to eyeball the ape man who sat in the Avery-McKnight living room than to give good wishes. They told him that they hoped he would come to church and find God.

Sometimes, after waking in the woods from a dream in which the God that he knew, which came only in dreams and only in the form of an orangutan or a gorilla or something more evolved than those but less evolved than himself, he would allow himself to follow the line of inclination left over and sit at the edge of where the woods ended and the rest of the world began. In winter, he could see where the grey frost crept but did not touch their domain. Where they lived, it was always warm and green.

It had to be around the time that the children decided to stop talking that they also decided to stop playing War. And it was around the time that they stopped talking and stopped playing War that the fine hair thickened, first on their arms and legs, then all over, until they could rely on it to hide themselves from each other. Allred was glad of it, being the shyest, and he thought the others felt the same. That was when their hands lengthened and their feet shifted. They had, at last, adapted.

Why, then, had he left?

He gritted his teeth, spat, and struck himself in the jaw with his nine-year-old's fist.

He tried again to open his mouth because to smell was also to see and hear. His mother always had seasonal allergies and her nose was stuffed much of the time, and nothing had changed in twenty years. His stepfather's sense of smell had been steadily declining and was now almost gone, and he commented sometimes, before and now, that he could only taste very strong things anymore, like Stilton cheese or ghost pepper salsa or those horrible Greek sardines that were packed in oily, salty garlic and stunk up the house. He surprised himself at how sorry he felt for them. More than that, it made sense, that furtiveness that cause them both to misread and thereby color everything according to their own disquietude. Everyone was out to get them. Everything was a threat. You could not read faces, you had to assume.

On the bench that commemorated his vanishing,

he kicked off his shoes. They were his old sneakers, black Vans with curves white stripes on the side, and they rolled down an incline, striking a trash can. Allred Avery-McKnight could hardly smell the grass. Panic came. Rather than face it and allow it to wash over him, because it would, he knew, eventually pass, he fell back on what his most recent ancestors did in moments of doubt: He stewed and he thought of whom he should blame for this and that and everything.

In the dark, his eyes glowed, but as it was, he could hardly see a thing.

Their mother inside, their father secreted in the study or the garage or the basement, the girls knew that the three of them had the yard to themselves. The taller two deferred to the smallest one, for she knew what to do in any event.

The girl (Julian was the name of their pet, a hairless ape that was not to be confused with the dog, called Jules) instructed the women to remove their shoes. She communicated this by unlacing and throwing the Keds over one shoulder, whereupon they soared over the fence into the yard behind theirs. The women followed suit, and tossed their high heels into next door yards on both sides. The Jacksons would fish a Cole Hahn treaded pump out of their pool. The Herreras would come upon a Jeffrey Campbell wedged sandal on the roof of their garden shed. The

Bohannons would get a child's white Ked jammed in their lawnmower.

She wanted to see what they would do.

She wanted to see if they would follow.

They wanted to see if things could be as they were before.

Beckoning, the eldest Livingstone girl pawed at the sliding glass door so that it did not make a sound on its track. They blinked at the sudden, powdery darkness that came from the overhead lights and too-high air conditioning. Their mother was not in the kitchen. Their mother was in the TV room, taking a phone call.

The eldest and smallest Livingstone, as her younger and taller sisters knew, their parents hated a game that they would play. The eldest had called it Stalk. The objective was to keep just out of sight and reach of any reigning adult in the house. The objective was to create an atmosphere in which the stalked knew that you could see them, but the stalked could not see you. You, the stalker, could be anywhere in the house and could spring upon the stalked at any time. You had to give your prey the idea that you were faster than they and thus able to leap from ceiling to floor and disappear into the laundry chute before they could turn around. And when they did turn, at last, there you were, as though you had been trailing right behind the whole time. The Livingstone girls had played it with a bevvy of babysitters, some inclined to engage (Shari had been a good sport, as had Brittani), others not (Traci swore that her nerves were shot by the time Dr. and Mrs. Livingstone returned from dinner out and did not want to come back, despite her regular rate being doubled, then tripled).

You had to be completely silent. You had to give the impression of a haunted house.

Children and animals can climb. When their mother wandered back into the kitchen to observe the pot of beans on the stove, one shoulder crooked up to keep the phone to her ear ("—well, you know what, I think it's a little soon for a really big get-together, Val —"), the eldest was on the top of the fridge. The younger two, eager to play, their limbs a memory bank for the things they hadn't done in years, squatted atop the cabinets. They had a broad view of the kitchen. Their mother was none the wiser, so far. Mrs. Livingstone stirred and talked and numbly brushed at the air when one paw dropped down from above to graze at the ends of the hair on her crown. It was early yet in the game; any detour in air traffic might have been a fly. And, as the girls knew, the best way to play Stalk was to keep the stalked from knowing that the game was happening for as long as you could.

And while his wife moved from the stove to the fridge to the table and poked her head around corners and bid her goodbyes and hung up the phone and went back outside ("Where the hell is everybody?"), and while his daughters leapt from their hiding places and proceeded to find others on all fours like subhuman chaos, leering and unfeminine with the eldest shedding their jewelry (the emerald earrings he gave Susanna, the heirloom sterling cuff he gave Teresa) like junk, David Livingstone loaded a shotgun. And, keeping close behind, in quietest footfalls so as to keep them from knowing that he was just so far in their wake, he shouldered the weapon.

He hummed internally, *Dr. Livingstone, I presume...*

They knew that the three who left the woods had had different dreams, and that they could not speak for them or what they meant or what their motivations were for leaving. However, Mary Kathleen and Clare and Evander had had the same dream the night they left their beds and their homes all those years ago. It lasted all of three minutes.

A lifetime in three minutes. Perhaps less than that.

It began in carmine despair and ended in green ambition.

The first phase: In which they witnessed their collective demise, strung from vines on a verdant tree. They were unrecognizable. They were furred and callused and their necks distended from where the vines were knotted. They were missing parts. They were purple and black and still and passive, for they did not resist a breeze, like forgotten effigies. Such sights might have woken these children in their beds and the dream would have ended outright, were it not for the overwhelming sensation that there was more to come, that this rotting state was temporary, as they were owed a resurrection. The ichor was not gone, behold, the mold being chased away by healthy tissue. It was like watching the enemy retreat into the hills. As the dream operated in reverse, their limbs were, in fact, being regurgitated from the mourners mouths in strips, as birds vomit nourishment down their newborns' throats. Legs and arms were revived on, not cooking pyres, but cleansing flames and reattached.

The second phase: In which they climbed down from the tree and undid the knots and reconnected the vines to the branches.

The third phase: In which they observed where the splits in them had deepened. There followed an age of mimicry, at first in complete seriousness, then in jest. They played games and had rules. These were reflections of what they had seen in their old lives, but because the years crept up on them and gained momentum, faster and faster, their falling into old patterns became less deliberate and more a matter of muscle memory. They formed alliances, which rearranged themselves.

Alonso. Allred. Julian.

Then it was Julian and Mary Kathleen and Clare.

Then it was Alonso and Allred and Evander.

Then it was Julian and Alonso and Allred.

Then it was Evander and Mary Kathleen and Clare.

Then it was Julian and Evander and Alonso.

Then it was Mary Kathleen and Allred and Clare.

Then it was Clare and Julian and Evander.

Then it was Evander and Allred and Mary Kathleen.

Then it was Alonso and Mary Kathleen and Clare

Then it was Julian and Allred and Evander.

On and on in countless combinations until, before long, it was six individual children who had agreed to live together. From above, they shuffled in nonpatterns. It was never quite clear, even from the bird's eye view that dreams and hindsight alike provide, when these factions began, and when it finally reformed into the thing that they had not wanted in the first place: Boys against Girls. The rules prevented them from moving beyond that.

Their fur thinned and they played War and they played Stalk. In reverse, War had the look of a detangling, wherein the two opposing sides had worked out their differences and came to some sort of truce and left the battlefield with as much resolve as when they had come to it with sticks and vine netting and discarded bicycle helmets. Overhead, the sun observed the whole thing with a shrug and let the earth go about its business. As with War, Stalk took on the antics of a different game altogether, the objective being to walk backwards through the woods, with the catch being for the players in front to step into the exact places as the players behind them. As a matter of fact, at the beginning, they'd played a game just like that and called it Backward, and while viewing it backward it played out like Stalk. During this phase, they grew smaller and smaller. Their fur grew more and more sparse. They began to walk upright.

The fourth phase: In which they dressed themselves and told Julian that she was not the boss of things around here. Or, through the cyclops eye of a dream, this was what it looked like. The true flux of things would have shown them stripping their worldly garments and conceding all around that Julian should be the boss of things around here. Because she was the oldest by a few months, though they would not celebrate birthdays. Because she had a way about her that had always attracted people to her, those who wanted to see what she would come up with next, and those who wanted to test their limits, and those who were happy to live a life in which they would always be told what to do. They would forget what Gifted and Talented was, but its significance would carry into her unofficial chiefdom of their group. But as the situation was reversed, they were telling her that it didn't make a bit of difference and who was she to design their society, anyway. They decided collectively that there ought not to be a leader at all.

The fifth phase: In which they got to know each other. Mary Katherine and Clare and Julian were girls. Mary Katherine's favorite color was purple, Clare's green, Julian's yellow. Allred and Alonso and Evander were boys. Allred's favorite color was red, Alonso's blue, Evander's orange. Their surroundings reflected their palette in flora and fruit. They were all in third grade. They did not like to go to school. They did not much like their parents either, though all lacked the vocabulary to explain why. They simply declared them "mean".

The sixth phase: In which they came through the gate and into the green.

The seventh phase: In which they clung to the broad, auburn fur on the back of a large orangutan, the way they might have done had their designs not progressed and had they continued to live in trees.

The eighth phase: The orangutan telling them to WAKE. UP.

And the ninth phase, which could repeat from the start, ad infinitum, depending on the outcome each time. In which the dreamers woke from their beds, three with that knowledge, three ignorant of it.

The three who were aware of how it might end woke for perhaps the second or third or thousandth time. Their eyes bore an animal glow in the dark. Mary Katherine came to under a constellation of stick-on stars that shone a radium green. Clare pushed aside the tools of her bedtime ritual, the flashlight, the chapter book, that night's exegesis being volume nine of *The Zack Files, The Volcano Goddess Will See You Now*. Evander kicked at the balled socks that had to be excavated each morning from his blankets, which his parents would keep as relics, not so much in remembrance of him as proof that he existed at all.

They rose.

They avoided the hallways and stairs and went out their windows. The drainpipes and trellises were sturdy enough to accommodate them. They went to the end of their driveways, each closer to each other than they thought, and waited under the streetlamp, willing abductees waiting for a signal. When they got it, they started out, going past solid shut places, apartment complexes, markets, gas stations, restaurants offering dollar menus, martial arts studios until they reached the park. They used different entrances. They were all looking for the ape.

And if it did not end as it should, it would start from the beginning.

She (for she would not have chosen for herself the name Julian) had such agility. She knew that she (for she would not have asked to be named for an anchoress who cemented herself into a narrow cell in order to be alone with God) could do anything, so long as she set her mind to it. If she knew anything about God (and she did), it was that anything could be climbed and that anything could be a game and that the rules were subject to change.

She believed in God because she believed in herself. She was filled with smugness when it became apparent to her how few people truly believed in themselves, and thus, how few people truly believed in God.

Nothing would happen that she did not want to happen.

She told her sisters this and they dropped to their knees, for they were looking at thirty in the face and she was nine again, and all three of them were certain that it was so. Her sisters wanted to know what her secret was. They did not want to go to work or to school or to get married or divorced or have babies or win prizes or make fortunes either. They did not want to achieve anything.

She (for she had no name) showed them what to do. The idea was to eradicate all doubt, because doubt would lead to the distrust of your own limbs, and to distrust your own limbs would lead to imbalance, which would lead to spills. It was a matter of jump and then grab. Jump and grab.

They went all over the house this way. The sisters were as cats. They walked along bannisters and perched over the balustrade that looked over the foyer. From there, they leapt across to the alcove where, during Christmas, their mother ascended by ladder to put up the nativity in its thicket of decorative evergreens and blinking lights. For the rest of the year the space was occupied by an amorphous iron sculpture that their mother bought at a craft fair the year before her eldest went missing. It was long and wide with a woven motif, like the fragment of a basket, and they hid behind this when they heard a tap from below and a snap. The three of them giggled, listened for their mother, whom they heard clopping demonstratively now across the foyer. She must have known where they were, or at the very least, that they were not far behind. The eldest the younger two peered through the iron weaving, and it was all they could do to keep from exploding outright at the helpless old gal down below. Mrs. Livingstone (because that was who she was), in her sweater and cotton t-shirt and linen trousers, standing there looking all pissed off because she knew the joke was on her, hands on her hips, scoffing, saying, "Okay, what the hell is going on? This is un-funny, it really is." Waiting, sighing, saying, "Nobody's going to drop a water balloon or something on me, are they?"

And hardly those words were out when a brassiere landed flat on her head. The cups, size C, lay neatly across, almost like a Mickey Mouse hat from Disney, though it was leopard print. She looked up and met a bombardment of more clothes. The big girls balled blouses and shed sweaters and their mother did what she could to dodge them. Her youngest two were naked to the waist until they were not, when a pair of jeans flew past her shoulder and a skirt and pair of black tights landed at her feet. Their underpants, which were too thin and so close-fitting that they caused a need in both women to urinate frequently, went over the balustrade with resolute shouts from Teresa and Susanna that they would never wear panties again. The eldest Livingstone sat in gleeful passivity behind the iron and the girl mouthed the weaving for the coolness of it on her tongue. She was still clad. No overalls or tie-dyed t-shirts descended. Her hair kept its shape. Meanwhile, her sisters bounced on the ledge, their knuckles like extra feet, and hooted, makeup in heathen smears across their faces, their hair damp and spiky.

"And I thought," their mother said, "if you can't beat 'em, join 'em."

Mrs. Livingstone, having stepped outside of the usual order of things, launched a counter-attack. Teresa caught her mother's sweater in the face, Julian one slip-on shoe. Susanna, whom her mother had not seen naked since she was eight or nine years old, rocked on her heels and applauded, making her breasts jump. Teresa, who had not let another living soul see her undressed since leaving her last boyfriend, turned and mooned her mother and the house.

The three in the alcove beat a tattoo and chanted. At first, it was unintelligible, vaguely rhyming, and slurred from the drunkenness that comes from the excitement of the insane, the young, or the fauna. It was distinctly familiar to Mrs. Livingstone until she recognized it from a memory, initially a haze until it solidified and crystallized, and she had it: The three of them, following the leader who was Julian, a summer day with no activities on the schedule, day camp canceled, leaving her alone in a house of wild animals. The sky was a clotted grey and they were going to pray for rain. Never mind that the weather forecast guaranteed a downpour between two and three that afternoon. Julian assured them that their everlasting chant of "FUCK WHAM GODDAMN, BASTARD GO FASTER" was what broke the drought. And in a brief lapse of reason, Mrs. Livingstone was inclined to believe her. The garden was lush it a way that it had never been.

"They did no such thing," David Livingstone said, now as then.

Was that when he aimed his rifle?

"Yes."

Whom did he shoot first?

"My wife," he said. "Then Terri. Then Susie."

He'd only been around the corner. Anyone could have seen him at any time, if they inclined their heads just so. In fact, the snout of the shotgun was too long to be concealed and his arms did not have the strength as in past hunting days. When he aimed, first for his helpmeet, his hold on his weapon was awkward, and rather than striking home, which would have been her head, he got her in the shoulder.

Mrs. Livingstone was a smart woman. "I played possum," she recounted. "He thought he got me in the neck, you see, and stepped right over me. I kept my eyes half-lidded and let my jaw go a little slack. It's difficult to be a possum in the midst of all that commotion. I almost cried out when Terri and Susie hit the floor. I did gasp."

A greater clatter came when the sculpture fell, and this prompted Mrs. Livingstone to look her younger daughters in their faces, or lack of them, for her husband's aim was truer this time. There was very little there to recognize, save for a permanent retainer on Susie's bottom row of teeth, most of which were still intact, if the rest of her head was not. She concentrated on that single band of silver and tried to remember if it had really been a necessary procedure, since all it seemed to do was accumulate plaque and bits of food. There was a fleck of something caught there now, and when Mrs. Livingstone was not looking at the silver, she looked at that.

She was confused by the shower of glass, at first. In the alcove was a hexagonal window, which her husband must have hit in his quest for the prize. As for the prize, she was unharmed.

"She kind of flew across the alcove," Mrs. Livingstone said, positioning her hands in demonstration. With her left hand, she played Julian and brought the girl in an arc over the straightened fingers of her right hand. "--and over the banister and disappeared upstairs. David went up, and everything got quiet."

The house was built in such a way that one could make a loop going from the main staircase in the foyer and reappear again via a second, narrower staircase that led into the laundry room just off the kitchen. The kitchen was large and eat-in and was the first room that a visitor would see upon entrance.

"That's how I assumed she got downstairs again so fast," Mrs. Livingstone recounted, who had not yet dared to raise her head. She was unsure, now that she and her eldest were alone, of what the girl would think to do. In light of what had passed, it was entirely possible that the girl might eat her. Mrs. Livingstone read of it and knew about it, having perused articles in nature magazines and shocker pieces that were otherwise called human interest stories, and she knew that cannibalism was almost entirely, save for two or three cases reported on wild chimpanzee troops in East Africa, unique to humans. The grill, in the midst of everything, had not been turned off and threw out the charred smell of old steak and chop dinners. Mrs. Livingstone had also gleaned from her readings that human flesh tasted of pork. Her husband would return to finish one or both of them. Perhaps he would put one or both of them on the grill. She resigned herself briefly to her end as an old pork chop dinner.

Mrs. Livingstone said, "We are an absurd

species."

But rather than fall prey to that instinct that is almost entirely unique to humans, her daughter's face grew red and gathered toward her nose. Mrs. Livingstone had never seen Julian cry before, and she had no reason to believe that her eldest was capable. To see it was to witness water from a rock, a miracle. To hear it, the snuffling, the high, forlorn sobs, the hiccups, was to hear, if not the voice of God, then to know the echo. Julian had always been quick to laugh and made you the butt of jokes that only she knew. Mrs. Livingstone could never stand it, the idea of a grown woman being made a fool of by one no more than four-foot-ten with less than a decade of life in her, being made a fool of by a messy kid who went to day camp.

Mrs. Livingstone said, "Of all the times when I wanted to kill her myself. Of all the times when I thought about how I'd do it, when it would happen, and what an absolute animal I was for even thinking things like this. Of all the times when I was sure I'd be the one to burn this house down with everyone in it. All because the kids didn't want to try a new lasagna recipe. Or because David spaced out when I was trying to talk to him. It would happen because I'd be alone in the house with the four of them. It would be her fault because she had them all snowed. She'd be the first one to show disgust for the new lasagna. She'd be the one David was thinking about, her schooling, her little enthusiasms, his protégée. She was the most like him of the three kids. David thought it was some sort of flattery." She breathed. "Of all that. Wouldn't you know I'd be the one to kick the front door open a little wider for her."

Julian had whined, as she never had when she really was nine years old, "I want to go home."

Mrs. Livingstone said, "I know what she meant. And she didn't mean here. If I'd said it, I wouldn't have wanted to go back to my mother's house either. I know what she meant and I don't. I'm not sure where I'd go if I could go home. Someplace sunny, I guess, and warm. Someplace green. Nice place if you can find it. God bless if you can find it."

With her one bare foot, the other still in its slip-on shoe, Mrs. Livingstone reared and budged the front door that much wider. She heard footfalls from above and had to return to her possum's poise, and while she did not see her eldest leave for the second time, she swore that she heard her, her small bare feet and the whoosh of the door as it opened and its crash as it swung shut.

David Livingstone said, "I'm still not sure. What did I do? Won't someone tell me what I did?"

She padded down the sidewalk on bare, pink feet. There was the inclination that she ought to make use of her top limbs in order to move faster, but trying the quadruped's gait made her stumble, almost head over heels in a complete somersault. The pavement caught her cheek and grazed it from lip to lower lid in a rash.

She huffed, snuffled, resigned to sitting on her overalled bottom in the middle of the street proper, not on the sidewalk with its powdery chalk masterpieces of butterflies and ladybugs, its arrows directing guests up driveways to birthday parties, and hopscotch grids. There was roadkill on either side of her, a cat to her left, a squirrel to her right. In time, there would be an invasion of vultures. Already, overhead, they circled; their descent was a lazy one, and they left her alone because she was still very much alive. When they had finished with the cat and the squirrel, they would ascend into the low branches and wait in hope for a minivan, an SUV, a negligent driver, as they often did. They'd never had a larger meal than a deer, and a child would last them for weeks. Vultures went where the best food was. They strutted like reptiles; their heads were rubbery and bald, and they wagged together like a lot of exposed penises.

She took up a piece of concrete and hit one in the eye, and they scattered into the trees, leaving dirty plumage. She wiped her wet face against her shoulder, blue and green tie-dye smeared and rusty.

What no one seemed to understand was that she did not want to be the leader. It was only that it had always seemed that she should take up the position, a matter of course, since everyone else appeared keener to marshmallow around in indecision until she put her foot down. Another thing that no one seemed to understand: That it would be that much easier to marshmallow around. Imagine that, to go without expectant eyes and pauses, glances, waiting for her to give the order. Not that she would have been content as a follower. That, to her, was a fate worse than death. And what she could not seem to understand was how anyone else could be content to wait and see what someone else, what she, would think to do next. Now imagine that, if everyone could think of what to do next all on their own.

The trouble with that was a creeping mistrust. Too much of that was to live on the edge. It was like playing Stalk and knowing that while you watched, you too were being followed, as was the one ahead of the one you trailed, and on and on. How many times in the woods had their number come so close to that precipice? So precariously close, completely accidental? They might all have eaten one another, despite the garden, its eternal summer and immortal, fruit-bearing trees. They could smell it on one another, a dirty, acidic stink akin to blood or refuse, and when it came they could detect it, and when they could detect it, they went to their separate corners of the green and gold sanctuary to be alone. When they were alone, they slept and dreamed of the orangutan, the Greatest Ape, as they came to call it, who told them in its way to live gently. It told them to live gently or they would perish, as would the woods, folding in on itself until all that remained was the dead end of a hiking trail in a town park, barricaded by dry cedar and chain link fencing, a glance into someone's backyard, the splash of sour chlorine in an above-ground pool, as though the eternal summer and the immortal, fruit-bearing trees had never been there at all.

It occurred to her when she was really and truly nine years old that she could decide to leave at any time, to not merely vanish into the woods, but altogether. She knew that people's lives were cut short by car accidents, by choking, by electrocution via state sanction or in an effort to wedge a piece of bread from the toaster with a fork, by poisoning, again via state sanction or from the bad luck of sampling leftovers that were past their prime. It occurred to her that all of these things could be done through your own volition. It came as naturally and as inexplicably to her as the sudden urge to push her father over the edge of their then unfinished house. He'd done nothing to warrant being pushed. She had nothing to be unhappy about, nothing she could, at that time, put her finger on. Everything that anyone could want, she had: a roof over her head and food to eat, an education, people who looked after her and made sure that she did not look unkempt. She hadn't, then as now, the vocabulary for it. She had it better than some. She had it better than most. She knew that, then as now. It was one of her parents' phrases, "It could be worse." Sitting with a strange sort of blindness and deafness to the world around you, not quite knowing what was expected of you and falling short, mastering the game only for the rules to change at a moment's notice, collecting prizes only to see them buried in a basement, making friends but not really because you were meant to be in competition or because their company made you look less vulnerable, thinking that it was better to be the top dog because so long as people minded you it didn't matter if they resented, even hated you. It could be worse. It was exhausting. It could be worse. And that was where the comfort came in, of knowing that she could leave at any time.

Then as now, it did not quite touch the back of her neck, but it hovered less than an inch above, enough to make the hair stand on end like a hot, constant breath.

Annihilation was annihilation, whether it was of yourself or others.

Maybe that was why she went to the woods.

She kicked out her feet and cast her hands above her head and made herself a flat star on the blacktop. Someone was bound to run her over.

Someone almost did, a minivan, bulky oval and deep purple as an eggplant. She tasted the exhaust and felt the rush of forty-five-hundred pounds that would have come at her but did not, thanks to a last-minute swerve that caused the van to collide with a recycling bin on the sidewalk. The kinetic energy of forty-five-hundred pounds was still in the air, the anticipation of joining the cat and the squirrel in a pulped tableau on black tar, and her eyes screwed shut.

When she opened them again, she mistook the ladies who craned from above to be the vultures, come down form the trees to make sure she was dead. She could not have known them. She could not have known that they were the mothers of the children who had stayed behind in the woods, and they were. She could not have known if they had all been riding in the van together, and they had not. She assumed they had been, if she did not know who they were. They wore light clothes for the summer weather, t-shirts and linen trousers from the Gap or Talbots or mail-ordered from L.L. Bean. They adorned themselves simply, in opal earrings and turquoise pennants and birthstone rings in sterling silver crafted by James Avery. They bobbed or cropped their hair, streaked it, feathered it. Their faces were beaky, and she did not identify her companions in any of them.

If she had recognized them and they her, what might they have said to each other?

Where is my child?

I don't know?

You do know?

Yes, I do, but I don't want to tell you?

What did you do?

I didn't do anything?

Is my child dead?

I don't?

Is my child dead?

I don't know?

Did you kill my child?

No?

Yes, you did?

No, I didn't, but are you going to kill me, because only now my father tried to do just that and I wouldn't put it past you?

I don't believe you?

Nonbeliever?

I'd never do such a thing?

You don't know that?

I'm certain that I never would?

What makes you so certain?

God would never let me?

What do you know about God?

How dare you, what do you know?

Only a little more than you, as it turns out?

It was Evander's mother who drove the van, nearly flattened her. Mary Kathleen's mother went this way on her afternoon constitutional, with or without her pug or one of her toddling grandchildren on a leash. Clare's mother was getting the mail, now tucked under her arm, catalogues, Gap, Talbot's, L.L.

Bean, her driveway catty-corner to the scene of the almost-crime.

They did not recognize her, of course. They had not looked at the pictures of the other five children who had vanished those two decades ago, only their own. And they had no reason to think that the girl before them could be anyone other than a neighborhood kid; her clothes, overalls and blue and green tie-dye, were no different than the fashions worn back in the day as today. They knew that because she was a child, she was supposedly precious, as was the code of sanctimony semaphored among the species. Children are precious because they are new and small, and it is the responsibility of the grown person to ensure their safety. The world, to a child, ought to be a sanctuary. They knew, too, that because she was a child, she was stupid, not handicapped, and willfully so to lie in the street as she was doing and inconveniencing everyone. Children are stupid because they choose, against their natural common sense and the teachings of their elders, to create chaos for no other reason than to see what will happen, to see how you will react, and it is the prerogative of the grown person to exercise their place on the food chain. The world, to a grown person, is a wilderness and if you cannot hack it, then you deserve a lashing, by the rod or the tongue. If Evander's mother had run her down, it would have been the girl's fault. If no one else had seen her, the blame would not be theirs. They (with a shamefaced glance toward God for mercy at the thought) might have been more patient, with the girl and with themselves, if she had been struck.

They were about to start in on her in this way, scoffing and henpecking, once they had asked the prerequisite, "Are you all right?"

Mary Kathleen's mother asked, concern underwritten by exasperation, "What happened to your shoes, young lady?"

The girl found her mobility and used it to scrabble away in a backward crabwalk. The vultures in the trees sighed; she would live, after all—another meal missed. She began to hiss, at them and the mothers. Her teeth were baby teeth but for those that were missing. Her rapping jaw, combined with the gaps, gave the impression of fangs, though what she had was square and loose in her head.

Clare's mother repeated the inquiry, and Evander's, now with more fire, an interrogation, a condemnation: "Where are your shoes, young lady?" The girl's soles were soft and the flesh was red from the hot asphalt. Blisters had risen and one now popped and oozed. She kicked at the women and spat. They pursued and chanted, "Where are your shoes, young lady?"

When she was a child, not now but many years ago, she thought that if she could imagine herself so intently, she could (and very likely would) become the thing that she pretended to be. It was always a dangerous precipice, that she might transform and become permanently fixed as a panther, a prairie dog, a monitor lizard and thus face eternity in her new shape. Not that she would have minded a life as any of these things. The horror came from the idea that she should remain among these people, in this neighborhood, to be an expert on the ways of her changed form, in addition to the expectation that she continue to uphold the customs of her old, discarded humanity. It would be awful, for one, having to brush her overlarge fangs as a panther; she would go through a tube of toothpaste a day. As a prairie dog, she would be chased by the very children who had resented her charism on the playground, for they would only be too happy to catch her and skin her alive, make her pelt into a tiny hat. And the life of a monitor lizard would be a lonely one, for the venom in her teeth would prevent anyone from wanting to kiss her ever again. She had always been glad to have stopped herself short of a true transformation, just this side of scales, fur, and tails.

She never quite knew why it was that she wanted to become an animal. It was not so very different, as it turned out, than what she already was. If she were a panther, a prairie dog, a monitor lizard living here and bound to these customs, still she knew that there would forever be that barking demand, "Where are your shoes, young lady?"

Imagine, a monitor lizard wearing shoes.

Imagine, a prairie dog memorizing the phobias.

Imagine, a panther reciting the Pledge of Allegiance.

Imagine, a child knowing what she knew.

And though these ladies who stooped and pecked and cawed overhead did not understand it themselves because they did not know the girl, they would have said, had anyone asked them, that they would have given anything to become a child again. These ladies were eons removed from that shape, that era, wherein time moved slowly, then, without warning, accelerated. A summer was an age, that lost civilization of frothy green trees and living bodies of water, bright colors and fruit, though oftentimes they were popsicles. These mothers looked back, not on their college or high school glories, but the free-range myth of the days when they played in the street. And a myth it was. What they did not understand and refused to remember were these minor but deadly inquisitions, crones gnarring, "Where are your shoes, young lady?" They would have asked, if anyone told them that it was possible, "Why wasn't I changed, too?", remembering living bodies of water, popsicles. A pardon from doing taxes, marriage counseling, osteoporosis. It would be akin to the Resurrection, which is to say a second chance.

Imagine, a grown up playing in the street.

Why does she get to and not me?

Then, think of it: The absurd occurred. We are an absurd species, as Mrs. Livingstone said.

The absurd: A negligent driver, not yet eighteen, piloting the eggplant purple minivan gifted to her by her parents for a high school graduation present, identical in every way but the license plate to the vehicle that had narrowly run down a willing girl sacrifice, came barreling across the intersection. There were the remnants of green and gold lettering on the rear window, a message commemorating the driver's senior year. The driver herself was invisible, having ducked out of sight to retrieve the phone that fell under the passenger's seat. She had wanted to change the song from MF Doom to Alan Parsons Project, "Coffin Nails" to "Games People Play". The ladies, whose only clue to their collective end was the kinetic energy of forty-five-hundred pounds kindling the air, would have said, had they seen the vehicle, that the minivan was operated by a single hand at the wheel, no body, like Thing out of *The Addams Family*. If the vehicle had not collided with one, two, three of the ladies whom she had not seen, the driver would have changed the song again, "Games People Play" to "Blank Space", Alan Parsons Project to Taylor Swift.

The girl, who was a child and untouched, was still and so was the scene: The ladies cast along the asphalt and flanked by the cat and the squirrel, the eggplant minivan whose engine muttered and whose stereo still played, not MF Doom or Alan Parsons or Taylor

Swift, but Todd Rundgren. In the confusion, the playlist had jumped three songs ahead. When she looked, the girl saw that the ladies had been knocked directly and neatly out of their shoes; the three pairs, all flat and easy slip-ons, were in only slight disarray, not far at all from where the ladies stood in them. Never mind the brains or the blood. Nor did the driver, when her head popped up, register the brains or the blood. She blinked and spit the end of her ponytail out of her mouth. She took in the child at the lip of the sidewalk, the three pairs of women's slip-on shoes, "Change Myself" playing midway through the second chorus. The impact of the van had scattered the ladies to either side of the road, and so the path ahead was clear. Never mind the streaked gore. Owl-eyed, the driver found her phone and changed the song again before lurching the vehicle forward, "Change Myself" to "Seven Days in Sunny June", Todd Rundgren to Jamiroquai.

Save for the child, no one saw a thing. It might have been an act of God, which is to say an act of nature. Amidst cracked bones and viscera, there was still the odor of chlorine, a summer day, Jamiroquai. *Class of 20*—something in green and gold graffiti would come off, along with sanguine fluid, under a garden hose with a little soap. Even in civilization, life went on.

The child left as the buzzards descended, rejoiced, and feasted on the nonbelievers.

The GP Paul found himself in a restless state and repeated that after-hours rambling of his younger days, when he was newly divorced. As during that time, he carried a bottle under one arm and sipped at five-minute intervals. He moved along the commercial drag, under orange and red and yellow lights in the shapes of burritos and burgers and sushi, a tire outlet that had twenty years ago been a Blockbuster, a Barnes and Noble that was now an Apple store. None of this was here when he settled in the area.

There was an apartment complex, with angular roofing and chrome accents, where a little limestone cottage was once a fixture, a signal that this was where you turned off to get to the office. To new patients, he would point it out when giving directions, the little limestone house in the vacant lot by the CBD dispensary and the JuiceLand. No one lived there, it had been empty for ages. Paul had it in his private mythology of the places he lived that it was the site of something, not exactly sinister, but recondite, like the ruin of a temple. It was a habit of his since he was a boy, to invent and assign a grander history of deserted places than their original purposes would have allowed: abandoned houses, dusty storefronts where new businesses had yet to move in, grassy lots with perfect, bare dirt impressions of former establishments that had been scraped away. If only you knew the incantation, or if only you were pure of heart, only then could you access its full majesty. You might open a portal. You might summon the hand to guide you through. The graffiti did not illustrate the presence of a gang or juvenile delinquency, they were runes. Those who slept there were not transients, they were pilgrims who had arrived at last. They had made their presence known, conveyed their unsullied nature, having weighed their sins and virtues on the golden scale with good deeds outdoing and negating their far fewer transgressions, said the words, taken the hand and gone forth to that Paradise, never to return.

Paul crossed and went to the place where the limestone cottage had been, now the lobby of the Hunters Chase Deluxe Apartments and Condominiums, and wondered if he should, even on the blacktop, in the middle of the parking lot, leave some sort of offering. Just in case. Should that hand touch down and graze his head.

"Humans are the only animal that engages in magical thinking," he said.

And it was true. Dogs did not wish for an afterlife or a body-and-soul assumption. If they had been left, they wanted only the return of their masters.

He, too, had played at being an animal when he was small, in much the same way that he conjured legends of abandoned places. In his fantasies, the boy Paul went hands-and-knees around his house and yard in imitation of some beast, never specific, though vaguely human. The idea did not seem to be transformation (he did not want to be a panther or a prairie dog or a monitor lizard) but a relinquishment of old habits. It implied a starting-over, that if he could master this new, unmolded, almost idiot shape, he could perfect it, as time went on, into what he was meant to be all along.

When asked, Paul flushed, shrugged, and said, "I was never the kind of person who stuck to my guns. I went with the crowd. I was told I ought to pursue medicine, I did it. I was told I should settle down here, I did. I was supposed to get married, I did. I'm supposed to have friends, I have them." These were traits characteristic of animals. "That's true. Herd mentality. That comes with other things. Dominance. Territorialism. Predation. Submission. I'd like to think that we're made of better stuff than that. I'd like to think that we can do better than climbing to the top of the food chain. You absorb the habits of everyone around you. You follow commands." He swallowed. "I'm sorry. I'm not entirely with it. I plan to go to my first AA." He drained the bottle and placed it in the square middle of the complex's parking lot, observing a moment of reverence before taking it back and tossing it into a dumpster. "Now that that's done."

Onward and forward, out of the parking lot and toward the curve of a residential street. The houses were brick and limestone, knotted in cul-de-sacs, and interspersed with grassy lots put there to accommodate the concrete drainage ditches that wound around the neighborhood. Paul stepped down and followed one of them, the leaves catching the hems of his khakis. The concrete was dry for much of the summer and he walked awhile in the valley until he came to its end at the city park's north entrance. Here was where folks came if they wanted shade, for there were many breathing trees, and here was where folks came if they wanted to play tennis. The park was considered property of the neighborhood association, and privileges extended to those who lived within a three-mile radius, including use of the tennis courts, the pool, the dog park, and the athletic fields. This was the side without parking, not for visitors. Paul went through, though he did not live here.

Had he ever wanted to be a kid again?

He started.

The question, repeated.

He went to a bench, the farthest one from the smelly block restrooms, stretched. It was evening and the air was less full of gauze, now that it was getting dark. He took the opportunity that came with a thin, cool breeze to remove his shoes, then his socks, something that became increasingly outmoded in all his years, in which he'd accumulated the various customs, one of them being which articles of clothing it was appropriate to remove in public. If Paul the GP were to have his way, he would have, most definitely, stripped to nothing, more than King David had done when he paraded the Ark of the Covenant through the streets. He would not own anything. For now, he concentrated the imagined relief to his bare feet on the grass. Grinding his heel into the gravel, ignoring green glass bottles broken into gems that cut to issue a welcome shock. It made him sigh.

"Maybe not the kid I was," he allowed. "Not that I'm saying I deserved *The Wonder Years* or anything like that," he added quickly. "I'm not complaining. I had it pretty good, pretty darn good. Better than most. You know that." He addressed, seeing and knowing as he now did for the first time, no longer alone. He was not afraid and did not need the consolation that came with such a discovery, *Fear not.* "I want to be looked after, I think is what I mean. No strings."

When he was a child, he played like a child, in that, he had an imaginary friend, who was his Lord or his Lady and his Maker and his God. Would he have called this being his Master, too?

"My Jiminy Cricket," he said.

When he was a child, he thought like a child, in that, he absorbed everything with his eyes and his ears and his nose and his tongue and his fingers and toes. Today, his sight, though influenced by corrective lenses, was still good enough to drive by without them. His hearing, though diminished by his younger days of listening to Steely Dan at top volume through noise-canceling headphones, did not require aids of any kind, not yet. His sense of smell was not as keen as it used to be, but he could pick up the change in seasons, and he could taste almost everything fully, though he knew it was best to narrow his food portions, now that his metabolism had slowed.

"I'm not as picky as I used to be," he said. "I used to put ketchup on everything when I was a kid, if I didn't think I'd like it."

Anybody could have picked me up and taken me away. Now, I'm the bigger one. I'm the one with the answers. I am a doctor. Fear not, I am a doctor. Believe me. I can tell you anything, provided that you are smaller than me, and you will follow. If not, I can do just what I feared most from anyone larger than myself. I can pick you up and take you away.

He did not say this aloud, but he knew that he was heard.

What if he were to articulate those things that manifested, thus far, in images? These things he could not put into words. These things were what followed the picking up and taking away, what it would mean and how it might feel. The definition of a predator was the larger picking on the smaller. A predator had a lair. A predator went on doing what he did because he quickly forgot any other method of survival. As his longtime friend Donna Avery-McKnight had said, it was not sexual, though to say that it came from the groin would not be untrue. Here was the place where real hunger was felt. The phrase should not be "Go with your gut."

Paul the GP did have this to confess. "Once, a year or two into my marriage, my wife was very sick with the flu. She slept most of the day for close to a week. There weren't many things she could do for herself during that time. It was left up to me to get her into the shower and brush her teeth, all that. She was pretty out of it."

He would not elaborate, knowing that it would be of little use, knowing that the pleasure of having a living breathing body dependent on his care was underwritten by the surefire thrill of being able to do what he wanted with her at any time. He bit her nails for her and swallowed hangnails and other fragments. He licked the crumbs from her eyes before she woke and turned them into kisses as she surfaced. He was like a dog, jealously guarding a favorite bone. In the guise of worry for her diminished immune system, he had their groceries delivered and ordered the folks from HEB to place the bags on the doorstep and to leave directly after they'd knocked. The possibility of adding something potent to her meals, or of gradually reducing her portions of soup and toast nagged at him, but a preternatural sense of decency (or the growing threat of supernatural intervention) kept him from doing that. He sulked when her fever broke and she returned to work.

Reasoning that he had held fast to his oath of doing no harm, he did not allow for more thought of that time, and in burying it, he was convinced, up to now, that his wife, now his ex, had no memory of those six days under his care, save for the illness, his devotion. There was Earth, Wind, and Fire on a loop because it had helped her sleep. He'd been a good husband.

What had she tasted like?

Paul said, "Stop it."

What was her name?

Paul said, "She didn't have one."

She did not have a name?

Paul said, "Not during those six days."

It was getting dark. Parkgoers chased the last rays through the entrances with one or two straggling packs. These were young people, high school kids and college kids, who made plans to meet at the basketball court or the birdhouses, for the exchange of numbers, kisses, sips of something, huffs of this and that, cash for pills and powder and fungus. They came hooded, like old-time devotees of a horned god. There were whispers, smoke, mutters, incantatory. Paul the GP thought he knew a sliver of a face who might be a neighbor. He held up a hand and canted it back and forth, and a fan of fingers waved back from the end of a flapping sleeve. Whoever it was turned back to the little gathering. There was a whinny, a wheeze, a panting, a snuffle, a sneeze. When all the trades were done, they leapt, long-legged, over the chain link and into the yards that backed up to the park, and a trio of deer that came down from the real woods followed suit to yips of surprise, delight.

"Stef, don't try and pet them."

"I did it once before."

"You'll get rabies."

"Deer don't get rabies. They're not dogs."

"Exactly, they're not dogs."

"Well, there they go. Good job, now you scared them off—"

They were two does and one buck with a proud rack that was shedding its velvet in ribbons. Here was the horned god and his harem of two.

Everyone long-legged wandered away and the noise petered out and the deer jumped the fences, and Paul the GP thought himself to be completely alone for no more than a solid minute.

When he was a child, he was nocturnal. He was awake, though he slept. There were nights in which he kept watch until he caught himself nodding, and dreamed himself readying for the day, pouring cereal, brushing his teeth, wandering out to the bus stop in a neighborhood that was familiar if not his own, with people he knew if not from school or temple or camp or the cul-de-sac. He dreamed a thousand years (though it was but four minutes) and spoke fluently in languages he'd never heard and learned things that were not covered in any curriculum offered by the Phillip D. Andermatt school system. And after a lifetime of education and observation, he gathered his shoes and his knapsack and his books and took the bus back to the curb at his very own driveway, went inside, climbed the stairs, dropped his things at the foot of his bed, undressed, wrapped himself in the evergreen flannel sheets and down comforter, and woke to the first slices of light through the venetian blinds.

Did Paul want to go back?

He said, without much hesitation, "Yes."

If he could go back, would he?

And with only a bit more hesitation than the last time, he responded, "Yes."

What made it any different than the place from which he'd come? Its appearance and location changed every time, though it began the same way: The morning routine, boarding the bus. Once, he passed fields of sunflowers. Another time, he was driven over a land bridge, crossing a wide, shallow body of water that spanned from horizon to horizon. The bus stopped in a neighborhood of Victorian houses stacked at an incline, like Telegraph Hill in San Francisco. Or it let him off in the cobbled square of a European city with a huge astronomical clock fixed in its central tower, like the one in Prague.

It was important to note that he'd seen pictures of all these places. It was also important to note that he had never traveled out of the country, as much as he'd wanted to. He identified the taste of the air, more so the odor.

What had he learned there?

Paul the GP said, "I don't remember." Then, "I was always under the impression that it was some sort of toy town. You know, that the San Francisco hills and the Prague clock tower were approximations of the real things. Very keen ones, almost exact replicas, right down to what the places smelled like. I was being picked up and taken to a fake San Francisco and a fake Prague. And I was being taught things, but that never seemed like the objective. I think the idea was that I was the one being observed. My absorption and reaction and adaptation was being recorded somewhere. Maybe I was in a laboratory and I wouldn't have been the wiser. One thing I don't think I paid much attention to—" he ducked his head, embarrassed. "One thing I don't think I paid much attention to was that everyone there was naked. Except for their shoes. It wasn't such a big detail at the time. Everyone has that kind of dream, don't they, where they're at school or in line at McDonald's or somewhere and they realize they forgot to get dressed." He paused. "But with that particular dream, you're bare head-to-toe. That's the narrative, across the board. You never have your shoes."

He said, "I wonder now, if I'd left my shoes, if I would've been let to stay there."

Did Paul the GP want to be a lab animal?

He said, "I worked with a trio of capuchin monkeys when I was in medical school. We used them for research in the treatment of dementia. Physically, they're not much different at all from us, and their ability to forage and use tools indicates another similarity, in terms of memory development. We measured the development of plaque in the brains of mature capuchins. After they'd expired, of course. We had a habitat for them that simulated their natural environment. We fed them accordingly."

They were a Colombian white-faced capuchin and two tufted capuchins imported from Trinidad. The researchers called the white-faced female Genie and the two tufted males Victor and Peter. They lived in a prefabricated enclosure that the research team furnished with potted cuttings of eucalyptus that grew greenly enough to create a canopy and put in a floor of mulch. The subjects' diet was a steady one of melon and oranges and bananas and sweet potatoes and pineapple and the pith of their rinds. For the days that they were given walnuts, the capuchins used the rocks that came with their meal to crack the shells. Their captors taught them many things, including the recognition of words and the following of commands. By the time that signs of dementia were clear in manifestation, though the subjects forgot much of their training, they did not appear to forget their captors, who had been kind to them. There was a photograph of a young Paul feeding a piece of pulped strawberry to Peter, mouth-to-mouth. Film footage showed the GP, then a scholar at twenty-five, directing Genie to turn off the floor lamp installed outside their enclosure, then Victor to turn it on again. Archives held data collected of the subjects' sleep patterns, wherein the capuchins were knocked out with small doses of ketamine and hooked via electrodes pasted to their heads to a spindle machine that recorded their brain waves. When the capuchins died, Genie at ten, Victor at thirteen, and Peter at fifteen, their brains were removed to determine the development of plaque content.

Paul the GP said, "They had a better life, I think, than most people get."

How would Paul like to live in an enclosure?

He said, "I think I might. If I were fed every day."

Imagine, capuchins feeding close relatives pulped strawberries mouth-to-mouth.

Imagine, a chimpanzee's paw guiding a toy bus along a play-dough road to collect close relatives at a Lego curb.

Imagine, an orangutan observing its close relatives in a simulation of what should be their natural habitat.

Paul the GP said, "I'm not even sure what my natural habitat ought to be. I'm just going through the motions to pass in this one." He stopped. "No, pass isn't the right word. To make it, is what I mean. To make it in this one."

He reached behind him to feel a paw and drew back a hank of orange, dreaded fur in strings. He held it to his nose to breathe in the musk, which was wholesome and dirty and delicious, and put the ends in his mouth to taste it.

When he looked behind him, he found himself alone again, save for the far-off commotion of a scuffle. It was not an adolescent disagreement or the overpowering of a loner by a thief or a molester, though, if Paul the GP were truthful, he might have quit the park in either event. The noise was not quite animal; he could tell this by its inarticulation, noises over words in protest, at first quiet so as to keep the fight contained, then rising without warning into voluptuous whining and throaty growls, which are sounds that children make when they do not have the vocabulary to describe precisely what it is they feel. Vexation. Alarm. Despondency. And something that they might have called hunger if an adult were nearby to tell them to use their words.

Paul the GP was an adult. Pocketing the orange fur, he left the bench, abandoning his shoes, and followed the pandemonium. Crossing the softball field, beyond the birdhouses and the playground and the tennis courts, around the bend on the gravel path to pass the pool, and over the tended banks of wildflowers and sinking into a wide expanse that was marshy during the rainy season and now overgrown with maximilians, Paul waded in golden petals up to his knees toward the noise. This was a portion of the park that was left alone by landscapers and it was unclear if it was owned by the city. From the houses on the hills, the windows were yellow and flickering, and when they went out for the night, the air you breathed was, for a heartbeat, thick and black. The streetlamps from the park had extinguished minutes before, one by one, down the paths. It was when you had adjusted to the light of the moon that you felt confident in putting one foot in front of the other, as Paul the GP did now.

The terrain was unfamiliar. In spite of the dry spell, his bare feet sunk every alternate step, into mud or excrement, and it was necessary for him to travel with one hand reaching ahead, for even here there could be a rise in the landscape. There could be a root underfoot and he would need this mendicant's hand to break his fall. There could be another stranger.

He knew that there was a copse of trees that during the day stood out like an island among the maximilians. It was important to note that his ears worked, for his sight as yet did not. This was allergy season and, in addition to their poor adjustment to the dark, his eyes were full of thick hay-fever tears, brought on by the pollen. He willed himself not to sneeze, cursed quietly when he did, and in that instant the varmint noise seemed to have stopped. But he plugged his nose to the next sneeze, and the ruckus started again, and his ears were keen enough to work out that if he kept going in a straight line, the volume would grow and the closer he would be to its source.

The distance was precise and closed in fifteen steps, and it was on the sixteenth that Paul the GP felt a change in the space around him, having gotten closer, the air that much more concentrated, like water, and his swollen nose allowed for the barest trace of vegetation, suggestive of living vines and moss, and he knew that he had not merely reached the copse, but breached its flora. He was in the thick of it. And it was here that he realized the full advantage of his senses because here, too, was the scene of the pandemonium. He called it pandemonium for the certainty that he had crossed many demarcations to come to this place, which was far removed from nature as he knew it to be. It was recognizable, he gave it that, and he peered at the confusion happening in the dirt through his runny eyes that he had to rely upon, now more than ever. He absorbed impressions of movement as readily as he would complete action on a bright day.

In the copse, three children tore at each other. There were two boys and one girl. As for the children themselves, they did not appear to know who was who, by name or by sex, save that they were all of uniform height and strength and used what they could in defense (or predation). It was one against the rest, having come upon one another at the same place, at the same time, not seeing or smelling or hearing anything beyond what one could find to assault the other two. Paul the GP saw that their teeth were nubby in their heads, and a weak swipe of a pink paw to an apple-cheeked face easily loosened them. The children would pause in the fracas to spit them on the ground in phlegmy gobs, and when they were out of baby teeth, they gummed at one another with as much force as their jaws could muster. They left bloody rings on little arms and short necks. Their heads sat on their shoulders and they knocked them together to make hollow-ish sounds like coconut hulls being cracked. Under this, they hissed and roared and gnarred and sputtered. And under that, clothes coming apart, the rendering of cotton t-shirts.

Paul the GP thought of Liz Taylor's sniff in *Cat on a Hot Tin Roof*: "Little no-neck monsters." It was why he'd never had children of his own. Even when he was a youngster himself on the playground, it had always seemed that a game of Tag could become a grisly free-for-all, given the weather or a cross-eyed look at the wrong kid.

He was afraid of children. More than that. He was as afraid of children as he was of wild animals. Take it further. He was as afraid of children as he was of people.

Bear in mind that humankind's closest relation is the great ape. Remember that news story in Connecticut about the chimp that had been raised domestically, practically from birth, who spent the better part of his life taking his meals at the table from a high chair as a member of the family. He was his owner's baby, which was also to say that he was his mother's baby. And all it took was the visit of a friend to the house, long-time and familiar as an aunt, to detonate in him a carnivorous rage because he did not recognize her. The friend had gotten a haircut, apparently. This was enough to provoke the chewing away of her face, eyes, and most of her fingers; she looked like a burn victim, post-surgery. The autopsy showed he had Xanax in his system. A deeper dive into his past revealed that, a couple of years prior to the attack, he had run away into traffic and was brought home hours later by the state police.

Remember, too, the anomalies of the most advanced ape of all. These creatures were immortalized in film and invoked at near-whisper, as if to say the name Dahmer aloud might summon the bespectacled geek from the grave. Paul's wife had been a true crime fan. He'd sat through (how many?) documentaries that reconstructed, reenacted, and more often than not revered the vile goings-on of another ordinary guy. Ted Bundy was a law student and was, by all accounts, good-looking, well-mannered, going places. John Wayne Gacy was a member of the JCs and the Democratic Party and ran a profitable house painting business. Their neighbors refused to believe that these ordinary guys were anything but that, ordinary guys. It was easy to blend until it wasn't. There was always an arrogance that tripped you up during questioning or a smell in the basement. Paul the GP said, "This isn't normal", to Dahmer and Bundy and Gacy, to his wife's vegging out ("It's weirdly relaxing."), to his own deviations. Of course, he would never tell her that he'd wanted to see what would happen if he kept her sick. More, he would never tell her that, to him, in the span of those six days, she did not have a name. And still more, he did not want to know if he had, for her, ever been on the receiving end of that color of thought, black as a bottomless pit. He thought of this time and that time, little mysterious illnesses, usually following some argument. She was a nice, quiet gal, whatever her name was.

Violence did not have to be outright.

In the progression of the species, certain instincts mutated. What had been fright became thrill. What had been appetite became aberrancy. Predation and perversion became one and the same.

When did that happen?

Paul the GP, uttering wetly the physician's vows over his balled fist, looked into the copse, then shut his mind to it, to observe the gore at a spectator's remove, as per his training, and be without judgement or disgust so that he could make way for a blank, cooled, far-away curiosity. *I will abstain from all intentional wrong-doing and harm.* The hay-fever tears facilitated a kind of blindness, not complete, not the outer darkness, just this side of sufficient to send the world around him into a slurry void. His own voice, low and gobbling through his fingers, resonated over the din, if only unto himself. To say that he was calmed would have been incorrect. He might have called himself professional. He might have said, "It's weirdly relaxing."

He thought that this is what it must be to have truly detached. This is what it must be to succumb to the concrete idea that there is nothing more than this. To say with arrogance that there is no God. Paul did not mean the corporate, king-making lout full of hate. He invoked at the eleventh hour, when he might have said, "It's weirdly exciting", the eternal and ever-rising. He did not want to wait for a messiah. Who really does? He wanted to believe in connection, which is also to say compassion.

How rare that is among our kind.

But just as quickly, something changed, and the children were quiet.

As sight returns to the blind, hearing to the deaf, odors to a broken nose and taste to numbed buds on the tongue.

The two males, as if tapped on the head, started, as if woken, to find themselves bearing down on the female. The male (who was once Alonso) had her throat. The other male (who was Allred) had her braid in one fist and the torn-away green and blue of her collar in the other. They both had a knee on her, in her stomach or in her groin, and it was impossible now to imagine what they had been about to do to her. As for the female (once Julian), she brought her thumb away from the male's eye, the one without a shirt, and gasped when she was that the pressure from her small hand had caused it to purple so much that it had swollen shut. The other male, the one with the discolored eyes, asked if they were going to rape her.

None of them quite knew what that meant.

They puzzled.

To rape was almost to kill, wasn't it?

Yes, almost.

It was like eating.

The male with the discolored eyes then clapped his hands over his mouth, as if to choke down and swallow the ugly, blunt little word.

He and he recognized she. She recognized them, he and he.

They were as they had been at the beginning of their time together. They were small, half-dressed, bloodied, back in the woods.

They embraced.

They began to cry.

They each pronounced that they wanted to go home. It was understood that home was not the place that they had run from. It was somewhere they wanted to get back to.

"How do we do that?" Allred sobbed.

Julian kissed him and Alonso kissed him, and they

formed a line, Julian at the head, Alonso in the middle, Allred bringing up the rear. They listened through the vines and under the sound of late-night cars from the adjacent neighborhood. A hooting whoop resounded, mammalian, not an owl, from within the copse.

The children mimicked the sound and crept toward it. The female reached one hand into the leaves to pick wads of dusty, tangerine fur from the branches. She passed it back to her companions, who studied it, rubbed it across their lips and cheeks and under their noses. The hoot came again, thrice more, each from a different throat.

And following those, one more, though what differed this sound from the others was its uncertainty and its roughness. It came from the opposite direction. Its tone was awkward, as though its vocalist were embarrassed to have issued it, accustomed as it was to coherent language and speech.

As for the children, they were at a standstill. Allred, who had Alonso hand, pulled one way. Julian, who also hand Alonso's hand, pulled the other. No one knew which direction was forward. There ensued a tug-of-war over the male in the middle, who howled when he felt the strain of the back-and-forth yanking in his armpits. This quieted the female and the other male. Everyone's hands remained clasped. They looked around, all around.

From behind a cluster of vines, Paul the GP cupped his hands around his mouth tried a poor imitation of an ape's call.

The children peered and saw him, for it was evident that, presently, they saw in a way that he could not, with all of their faculties. Foremost, they smelled him. He could smell himself, a fusion of human funk, redolent of rectal emissions and open pores like open sores. He could not stop farting or sweating. To say that he could not help it had the note of an excuse, never mind that these were things that every living creature did.

Paul the GP waited for the children to attack and braced himself for it. When they did not, he came out from the green and stood plainly in front of them. And they, frozen mid-step in their trio, the female with one foot raised, fixed their eyes on him. Paul thought that it was not unlike the countless times he had gone walking in a park, this park and any park, or down the sidewalk in his own neighborhood, and coming across a deer emerging from some woodsy, underdeveloped part without houses. They would come down from the real wild to peck at birdseed in yards. The encounter was always the same: He would see them, they would see him, he might extend a hand, they would keep their position, absolutely still, until he took a step forward. His movement seemed to trigger in the deer the need to remember themselves and, like a spell being broken, they would come back to life and stride away, not really frightened, but cautious, knowing that this ordinary man was unpredictable.

Maybe if he thinks we're a bunch of lawn ornaments, he'll give up and go away.

And sometimes they did blend in with the plastic reindeer at Christmastime.

The children, bloodied and bruised and not breathing, linked hands and stood absolutely still. Eyes wide in their heads and luminous, the way that animals' eyes flicker in the dark in absorption of any light.

Maybe if he thinks we're statues, he'll leave us alone. Maybe if we don't move, he won't see us. Maybe if we don't breathe, he'll think we're already dead and he won't want to eat us.

Paul the GP wanted them to know he meant them no harm, because that was the key phrase in the Hippocratic Oath, the one everyone remembered. *First, do no harm.* He produced a token, pulled it from his pocket, held it up. He could hardly see it himself, just as he could hardly see the hand in front of his face or the hank of orange fur it held, and he envied that the three of them could. He had not been able to see in the dark, much less the blackboard, since he was in fourth grade.

They showed interest, made clear by their collective relaxation, their deeper breathing. He would not ask them where their shoes were. That was good. It felt as though they were very far from the park and the neighborhood or the commercial drag or the highway and any cars. And if they were at such a remove, it meant that time did not work in the same way either. They were in a pocket-sized microcosm, all aware that they were being watched by life without solid shape; Paul might have called it God. One of the boys, the one who had used the word before, used this lapse in time and place to ask if the GP was going to rape them.

Paul the GP sighed. "God, no."

The other boy asked if he was going to kill them.

Paul the GP said again, "God, no."

The girl asked if he was going to eat them.

At this Paul the GP laughed out loud, startling the children, and he backed down into his former stance, saying a third time, "God, no."

The children nodded, satisfied, if not trusting. The female came forward and reached for the hank of orange fur. Paul drew his hand back and closed his fist around it, and the fibers dripped between his fingers. He shook his head, back and forth, back and forth on his neck. He would have explained to them that he wanted proof, as much of something beyond the veil of modernity as of this night.

Paul asked the children if he could go with them.

The children traded glances and laughed, with more pity than conspiracy. Of course not. What a question. He did not have the skills or the nose or know the rules. He would remember the comforts of the internet and would spend eternity wandering in search of cell service. Food would go right through him in runs. He would wake every hour to relieve himself. Of course, he could not come.

He was sixty-eight. What a drag, what a bummer. He had to laugh, too. It made for a ridiculous picture, Paul, medical school graduate, number twelve in his class, going around on all fours and eating berries. It was a bit late in life to adapt to old ways. He'd been married, divorced. He had children who no longer lived with him. He knew the dictionary definition of the word rape. It was something bad that people did, he would say if asked. Could he go one day without looking up the weather, ordering necessities from Amazon, killing time by playing Wordle or Pokémon Go, or downloading the classics at ninety-nine cents per book with every intention of reading them? Could he really see himself eating pulped fruit, mouth-to-mouth, with his devolved companions? Of course, he could not come. And, with a heavier heart than he thought he'd have, though he knew its truth, he did not want to come.

From far off, another hoot, and another and another.

From here, the boy, the other boy, and the girl answered in kind. When they finished, they looked to Paul the GP with gentle snideness, as if to say, "*That's how it's supposed to sound*", in reference to his inexact attempt.

But they let him follow as they ventured out of the copse and into the maximilians. They did not let him hold any of their hands. If the flowers were knee-high on Paul the GP, they washed around the children's shoulders like waves. His eyes were still full of pollen-bred tears that leaked and stung him, and he had to rely on his ears, which, considering his tone-deafness from his ape-call, did not do much to absorb the sound of small, precise steps in front of him. He recorded snaps and whooshes and brushes and did his best to put his own feet where the children's had been. If he'd known about the game Stalk, this was a variation of it.

Under and over the trio of hoots was a rumbling, delicate, fresh as crystals. It was the sound of running water, though the river was on the other side of the park. The river was on the other side of the park and it curved away and out toward town, close to the library, where you could look out from the media room and see where it started, flanked in a straight line by cypresses before it turned again into a loop. They were receding from the library and the rest of the park and the houses. Paul did not look back. If he did, he feared (hoped?) that the expanse behind would yield nothing more than yellow petals for miles and miles, and because it was nighttime, the dark would facilitate that effect.

His reason insisted that it was on account of the

fact that he had never really been out after dark. Of course, he had been out late, a youthful bar-hopper until it made more sense to buy booze at the HEB and drink alone at home. There was a drunkenness that came with not knowing the territory, let alone where to step without falling flat on his face. It was a similar, giddy bliss, intoxication, to being a kid. Being high, being drunk. It smothered the past and future and put you firmly where you were right now, not caring, wanting to see how much further you could go. You might fall. You might vomit. But you didn't worry about it.

That was what it was to be a kid.

Ahead, the children were lighter by the minute. They laughed and their steps evolved to prances. They emitted more hoots in quick succession. Gradually, they would duck at intervals into the flowers and pop up again, still attached. Paul guessed that they were clinging to each other somehow by their clothes, perhaps by the teeth, or, rather, gums. It was during their brief disappearances that he had to stay put and wait for a burst of action somewhere far afield. He wondered if it were, in part, a deliberate maneuver to get rid of him, for far afield was more and more where they were in relation to where they'd left him.

It was when he was alone that he mustered the gumption to get his bearings and took a real look around. Indeed, at first, the flowers went on for miles until his eyes cleared and he could make out the shape of the copse in the distance. Should he be wary of muggers, even out here? The teenagers (how many of them had there been? Three?) would have been welcome company, and he was sure that one of them was a neighbor. If it was who he was thinking of, he knew her mother, who was a patient. They lived two houses down from him. He saw them at block parties and Christmas parties. He'd gone out for coffee with her, but nothing came of it, and there were no hard feelings, they remained friendly on the sidewalk and professional in the office.

God above, it was lonely.

Animals and children gravitate toward company. It was why you always saw them in packs and why the sight of a dog on its own or a cat on its own or an abandoned child struck such chords in the heart as to provoke real tears, not of allergy.

Joan Didion or D.H. Lawrence or someone like that said something about animals and how unacquainted they were with the preoccupation of their own sorrows. Paul the GP remembered it now: "I never saw a wild thing sorry for itself."

Merciful God, I am alone. Don't you see that?

As a kid, he never thought he'd say that, in prayer or out loud.

If he were an ape, the idea would never occur to him.

It made him run ahead and hoot, badly, sloppily. He ran and hopped to avoid pitfalls and humps in the earth, and it made him think of Judy Garland as Dorothy Gale and Ray Bolger as the Scarecrow sprinting through the field of poppies that lay between themselves and the Emerald City. He stopped because he thought that someone was laughing at him, not the children, but the teens, at how (forgive him this word) how faggy he must appear to them. Or how old. Or how clueless. No, how desperate.

Too, Paul the GP stopped at the outline of silver webbing in the air. A step closer revealed it to be a chain-link fence nine or ten feet high, a gate. He shook his head, to cast away images of huge, cinematic spiders. Did he really think he'd wandered into Jumanji? Here was a gate, this was a portion of the park that was undeveloped. The city had simply not gotten to it yet.

Paul the GP said, "I'd heard of plans being made with the parks department and at the town hall. I think, last I heard, they were going to build this part up and put in a rec center. I mean, the one we have in town isn't all it could be. It makes sense to put it out here—"

He didn't know who he was saying this to. He didn't know for what benefit. It was something a lot of folks did when they were grown, as if in rehearsal for any given event, any question that might be raised. Everyone prepared for cross-examination. You had to know what you were talking about.

Jesus Christ, can't you just be wrong sometimes?

Or just speculate?

Or, better yet, just not say anything at all?

It might have been that moment at which Paul the GP lost his marbles. A telltale sign of an adult who has lost their marbles is their conscious decision never to speak again. Another one is the spontaneous shedding of clothes. This he did, starting with his shirt, unbuttoning it as he progressed toward the gate, knowing how he would present himself, should any spectators catch him: A grown man undressing as children, thankfully unaware on account of their present laughter, skipped ahead. No one would believe him if he told them the truth: that it was a last-ditch effort to become one of them, that soon enough he would begin to shrink, the individual years fall back, then whole decades, and only when he had reached the beginning could he begin to advance, differently than before, reformed, if deformed.

He did not shrink, of course. He did not make that transformation because, if he were truthful, he did not have the energy to do it. Everyone wants to be a kid again until they realize what they lose. Instead, they all say something to the effect of, "If I knew then what I know now. And still had a full head of hair."

Paul had said it, too.

He paused in the undoing of the buttons and folded his arms across his naked breast, to watch the children fuss with the bar lock on the gate. They joined forces to wrest it open with a heave-ho until they got it open, where, beyond the chain-link and in the thick of endless green and the sound of clean, silver water where there was not supposed to be a spring, the hooting grew louder. He shut his eyes when he saw them disappear (the second time) over a hill, down and down to where Paradise was. If he kept his eyes shut, he reasoned that a miracle could be worked. Three children would meet another three at the bottom, all alive and well. As though nothing had happened, as is the way of a second chance.

When they were gone and the hooting silenced, he opened his eyes and it was several hours later. Anyway, it was within the first hour of daylight; he could see by his watch that it was just after seven.

Well. Paul (abandon the title here of general practitioner) remembered that it was Saturday. He did not have to be anywhere. His shirt was still at the halfway point in the unbuttoning project, and he continued until it was open and then off. He threw it over the fence, then his pants, his underwear, then his watch. Presumably, his shoes were where he'd left them, by the bench, and he hoped that someone would claim them at a later point.

He was bare now, save for the orange tuft. This he cupped over his penis for a thready loin cloth.

When he found the path again, the park was still empty, and he felt like the primordial man until a jogger with a trotting dog rounded the corner and he ducked into a bush until they passed. Coast clear, he stepped out, nodding at the memorial bench, and exiting through the one allotted to the neighborhood association. He bypassed the commercial drag because he did not think he could stomach the noise. Bare to the sole, his gait was stiff. He had never been undressed for longer than necessary, more and more, up to now, only for the time it took in the shower and to select clean clothes.

I don't want to bother with that just now.

There was a feeling of liberation with this kind of vulnerability. He'd had an inordinate number of nightmares that revolved around the search for his missing wallet or his missing phone. The terror was as thick as the horrors that came to him as a boy, in which he was chased by a woman with a face that looked like it had been pressed on a grill and that her injuries were somehow his fault. It was greater than the nightmares that came later, when he was in his teens, and featured that old trope of showing up at McDonald's naked.

I don't know where my phone is, or my wallet. And I don't care.

He sighed, and kept moving.

He was one male.

Now was the hour when the streetlights turned off.

He encountered no police cars, thank God. Thank God, for he had no hydrangeas with which to cover himself. Of course, no one had ever thought him dead.

There were no memorials for him to pick from.

And not for me a life everlasting. But I can pretend for a while.

Once called Paul, a man in the full nude stood on the sidewalk and watched the sun go up, the lights go off, the sprinklers start. It was Saturday and no one would emerge so early. Such is the sanctity of the Sabbath; you greet it when it comes and you salute it when it leaves.

He'd see how this went until sundown maybe, and take it one day at a time.

Not to his own dwelling he would go. He was not ready to face it and he did not want to be confronted by the phalanx of appliances and his own soap smell; it was a sharp three-in-one combination in a bottle, advertised for men, to be applied in a shower that he would have said years ago spouted the water too hot. It would be too much to jog the too-recent memory of how the faucets worked.

And so, he went a bit further down, where there was the flame of a TV going in the window. This was the neighbor he'd gone for coffee with, of whom he had no hard feelings. And for a single date, the woman had been at ease with the idea of telling him a surprising amount. He knew that she drank more coffee than water, or that was what she claimed. He knew that she'd had trouble sleeping, or she was at the time of their coffee outing, and thus developed a penchant for old movies, based on whatever Turner

Classic Movies had to offer, as it ran at all hours, a Jack Lemmon marathon followed by a Kubrick retrospective followed by a small-hours quartet of Hepburn and Tracy pictures and, after that, a parade of *Thin Man* movies. Her favorite had been *A Delicate Balance*, with Katharine Hepburn and Paul Scofield and Lee Remick and Joseph Cotten, directed by Tony Richardson sometime in the seventies. She said she remembered seeing it in the theater when it came out and found it funny to come across it again at three AM.

He wasn't a movie person. Perhaps that was why they hadn't hit it off.

He'd liked *Cat on a Hot Tin Roof*, and watched it at her recommendation. That ought to have been something. She hadn't been impressed and it had irked him at the time.

He stood now in the yard and let the sprinkler run over him thinly, up his legs and sagging ass-cheeks and over his more and more visible crown. From here, he could see that she was in her living room now, and what the TV was playing. Turner Classic Movies, from the icon in the lower right corner of the screen. It was *Who's Afraid of Virginia Woolf?*, with Liz Taylor and Richard Burton and Sandy Dennis and George Segal, directed by Mike Nichols in the sixties. It was black and white and hysterical.

She was absorbed.

She was alone.

Her daughter was, presumably, not yet home.

And so, he let himself in. Because the door was unlocked, because he was lonely. Because he might like this flick. He mouthed along with Richard Burton lines from the film. Maybe he had seen it, if he remembered this much. *Hark. Forest sounds. Animal noises.* He dripped onto the runner carpet in the foyer.

She started from the sofa, coffee mug in one hand. "Stef?"

Kathleen Benson, because that was her name, said, "I went around the corner and saw a naked man in my house. It took me a second to place who he was. Of course, I was afraid, either way. I didn't know what he was going to do."

Acknowledgements

To my parents, my brothers, cousins Amy, Gen, Katie, Hannah, Claire and Tory. To Nate at Spaceboy.

About the Author

Pam Jones was born and raised on the East Coast and now lives in Texas. She studied creative writing at Hampshire College. Her first book, *The Biggest Little Bird*, was published with Black Hill Press/1888 Center in 2013 and rereleased under the title *A Carnival of Birds* with Spaceboy Books in 2023. Other works of fiction include *Andermatt County: Two Parables*, IVY DAY, *The Joyful Mysteries*, *Anointed*, and *The Arizona Room*. Her short fiction has appeared in *The Cost of Paper* and *Boned: A Collection of Skeletal Fiction*.

About the Publishing Team

Nate Ragolia is a lifelong lover of science fiction and its power to imagine worlds more hopeful and inclusive than the real one. His first book, *There You Feel Free*, was published by 1888's Black Hill Press in 2015. Spaceboy Books reissued it in 2021. He's also the author of *The Retroactivist* (2017). His most recent book, *One Person Can't Make a Difference* (2022), was featured on Tor.com's Can't Miss Indie Press Speculative Fiction list, and was translated into Italian for Ringworld Sci-Fi in 2023. He founded and edited *BONED*, a literary magazine, and also created two webcomics. Nate is also a husband and a dog dad.

Shaunn Grulkowski has been compared to Warren Ellis and Phillip K. Dick and was once described as what a baby conceived by Kurt Vonnegut and Margaret Atwood would turn out to be. He's at least the fifth best Slavic-Latino-American sci-fi writer in the Baltimore metro area. He's the author *Retcontinuum*, and the editor of *A Stalled Ox* and *The Goldfish* for 1888/Black Hill Press.